ARCHIE IN THE CROSSHAIRS

ALSO BY ROBERT GOLDSBOROUGH

THE NERO WOLFE MYSTERIES

Murder in E Minor
Death on Deadline
Fade to Black
The Bloodied Ivy
The Last Coincidence
Silver Spire
The Missing Chapter
Archie Meets Nero Wolfe
Murder in the Ball Park

THE SNAP MALEK MYSTERIES

Three Strikes You're Dead
Shadow of the Bomb
A Death in Pilsen
A President in Peril
Terror at the Fair

ARCHIE IN THE CROSSHAIRS

A Nero Wolfe Mystery

Robert Goldsborough

MYSTERIOUSPRESS.COM

This is a work of fiction. Names, characters, places, events, and incidents either are the product of the author's imagination or are used fictitiously. Any resemblance to actual persons, living or dead, businesses, companies, events, or locales is entirely coincidental.

Cover design by Neil Alexander Heacox

978-1-4976-9041-7

Published in 2015 by MysteriousPress.com/Open Road Integrated Media, Inc.
345 Hudson Street
New York, NY 10014
www.mysteriouspress.com
www.openroadmedia.com

To Janet

ARCHIE IN THE CROSSHAIRS

CHAPTER 1

As nights in July go, it was as pleasant as New York offers, although my positive mood as I walked across town may have been because of my successful session with the cards at Saul Panzer's apartment on East Thirty-Eighth Street. A group of us play low-stakes poker there every Thursday, and I usually finish the games with my wallet somewhat lighter than when I start.

Saul is normally the big winner, although Lon Cohen of the *New York Gazette* usually comes away in the black, too. Tonight, though, both Saul and Lon were losers for a change, while Bill Gore did slightly better than break even, Fred Durkin had decent winnings, and I was eighty dollars to the good—my biggest payday in recent memory.

I smiled as I relived the well-concealed heart flush I was dealt in seven-card stud. Saul held a not-so-well-hidden jack-high straight, and he kept raising me, to his ultimate dismay. The biggest pot of the night, by far, rolled my way when the cards came down. Now, normally, I take a taxi home after these games, but the combination of the beautiful weather and the exhilaration of victory propelled me to walk the thirteen blocks west and then slightly south to the old brownstone on Thirty-Fifth Street that I have called home for more than half of my life. And besides, I needed the exercise.

My spirits were so high that I even violated a personal rule and gave a fin to a limping panhandler who was working the corner of Park and Thirty-Seventh. I had a good idea where he would spend the Abe, but at the moment, I didn't particularly care. All was well with the world.

As I entered the final block of my walk, I was vaguely aware of a car approaching from behind. *Probably a cab hauling a late-night reveler home*, I thought as I dug into my pocket for the front-door key. But before I could reach it, two gunshots pierced the night stillness, and I thought I heard an impact against one of the walls to my left. Instinctively, I dropped to the sidewalk as the car—it was not a cab, but rather a dark-colored Dodge or Plymouth sedan—roared away, tires squealing as it turned at the intersection and tore away into the night.

So much for my long-held perception that I possessed a sixth sense when it came to detecting approaching danger. I never saw it coming.

Slowly, I got to my feet and brushed off my pants. An upstairs window opened in one of the brownstones across the street that filled the usually peaceful stretch of West Thirty-Fifth Street. "What was that?" a hoarse female voice demanded. "Who's out there? What happened? You—are you all right?"

I ignored her and climbed the front steps, holding my keys with a shaking hand. But before I could reach the door, it swung open.

"Archie, what is happening?" said Fritz Brenner, clad in a bathrobe, his brow furrowed. "The shots . . . ?"

"That's what they were, no doubt about it," I said, swallowing hard and wishing I had something—anything—to drink. "Is Wolfe awake?"

Fritz shook his head. "You know him, Archie; he could sleep right through a hurricane."

"Well by all means, let him sleep through this, too. And don't tell him about it when you take him breakfast in his room. We wouldn't want to interfere with his digestion," I said, adding, "I'll fill him in after eleven, when he's finished his session with the orchids."

"Was someone shooting at you, Archie?" Fritz looked as shaken as I felt.

"I hardly think so," I said, trying, without much success, to appear calm. "Maybe it was some joy-riders who'd had themselves a snootful," I added, not believing my own words.

"But Archie, we haven't had any gunshots along here for years. Not since—"

"I know," I said, cutting him off. "Not since Arnold Zeck's crew machine-gunned the plant rooms."*

"But that was some time ago," Fritz said. "Maybe I should stay up and keep watch on the street."

"You will do no such thing. Nobody's coming back to shoot up the neighborhood," I said with a bravado I did not feel. "You need your sleep, and so do I."

With that, Fritz bowed his head and, with a mournful expression, turned to go downstairs to his room while I went upstairs to mine.

---

* *The Second Confession*, by Rex Stout

CHAPTER 2

The next morning, I took my breakfast at the small table in the kitchen as usual. Fritz dished up wheat cakes, cornbread, bacon, and orange juice, which I consumed as I paged through both the *Times* and the *Gazette*. By tacit agreement, no mention was made of the previous night's activities.

Once I was settled at my desk in the office with a cup of coffee, I opened the morning mail, placed it on Wolfe's blotter, and then typed up the correspondence he had dictated the day before. I had just finished all of it when I heard the *whirr* of the elevator just after eleven, signaling Wolfe's descent from the plant rooms.

"Good morning, Archie, did you sleep well?" he asked, as he does when he enters the office each morning.

"Better than I had any right to," I said as he settled into the reinforced desk chair—built to support his seventh of a ton—and pushed the button under his desk, the signal for Fritz to bring beer. He raised his eyebrows in response to my comment.

"Shots were fired outside the house late last night," I told him.

"I heard nothing."

"It has been said that you can sleep through a hurricane."

"Confound it, report!"

"Yes, sir." I proceeded to relate the events as he leaned back, fingers interlaced over his middle mound. When I finished, he came forward and opened the first of two chilled bottles of beer, pouring himself a glass and watching the foam dissipate.

"Do you feel you were the target of the shots?" he asked after his first taste.

"I don't know. I'm not aware of anyone in particular who has something in for me. I really haven't any—"

The phone rang, and I swiveled in my chair to answer it. "Nero Wolfe's office, Archie Goodwin speaking."

"I wish to speak to Mr. Wolfe," a high-pitched voice, likely male and probably disguised, responded.

"Who is calling?"

"I assure you, Mr. Wolfe will wish to speak to me."

I cupped the mouthpiece and turned to Wolfe. "Wants to talk to you, won't give a name." He nodded and picked up his instrument. I stayed on the line.

"Yes?"

"Nero Wolfe?"

"Correct. And you are?"

"My name is of no consequence. May I assume Mr. Goodwin is listening?"

"You may assume whatever you choose."

"I hope he is hearing this, because what I have to say relates directly to him. He is going to die."

"So shall we all, sir. What is your point?"

A snort. "You are being philosophical, Mr. Wolfe."

"No, realistic."

"Suit yourself. I repeat that Mr. Goodwin is going to die, and in the not-too-distant future. He could have died last night, but the time has not yet come. The shots, fired just a few feet from him, were off-target by design."

Wolfe's jaw tightened. "What is it you are intending to accomplish?" he asked.

"The killing of Mr. Goodwin, of course."

"Why?"

"As retribution against you."

"Should *I* not then be the focus of your animus?"

Another snort. "Easier said than done. It is widely known that you rarely leave your citadel, regrettably making you a most elusive target. Mr. Goodwin, on the other hand, is what might be termed 'a man about town.' Besides, removing Mr. Goodwin is a most effective way of neutralizing you. Without him, you are a crippled genius—if in fact you truly possess genius, which remains open to question. Oh, with Mr. Goodwin out of the picture, I suppose you could bring Mr. Panzer on board as your adjutant, although as crafty and clever as he is, I doubt the synergy would be the same. And if he did by chance become as effective as Mr. Goodwin has been, he too would be removed."

"A pretty speech, sir. Now I want—"

"That is all I have to say for the moment, Mr. Wolfe. We will talk again soon. Good day." The line went dead.

"He was afraid we'd put a trace on him, probably," I said. "What do you make of this?"

Before Wolfe could respond, the doorbell rang, and I went down the hall to see who our visitor was. I was not surprised to see the bulky figure of Homicide Inspector Lionel T. Cramer through the one-way glass. I went back and reported to Wolfe, who scowled and dipped his chin—the signal to let the inspector in.

"Good morning," I said as I pulled the front door open. "We were not expecting you."

"I'll just bet that you weren't," Cramer growled, barreling

by me and heading down the hall to the office uninvited—his *modus operandi* when he dropped in without advance notice, as was invariably the case.

Some words here about Inspector Cramer: He has been on the New York City police force since before I came to the city, and he has known Nero Wolfe longer than I have. When he comes to the brownstone, it is invariably because he is angry—usually at Wolfe, me, or both of us, and usually because he feels we are impeding the work of the police department.

The two men have a grudging admiration for each other. Cramer, for his part, knows damn well that Wolfe may be his best hope at solving a case; and Wolfe respects Cramer's toughness, bravery, and honesty—if not his volatile temper.

"You must be in the middle of something really hot," the inspector snapped as he dropped into the red leather chair at the end of Wolfe's desk, plugging an unlit cigar into his mouth as he so often does in his visits to us.

"After all these years, I should be used to your surprise visits and cryptic comments, but you continue to outdo yourself," Wolfe remarked dryly. "What brings you here today?"

"Hah! Playing dumb, eh? It doesn't suit you and never has. Care to comment on last night's activities on the street just outside your door?"

Wolfe drank his beer and dabbed his mouth with a handkerchief. "I don't have enough information to comment. Perhaps you can elucidate."

"You're damned right I can elucidate," Cramer said. "As if you weren't aware of it, at approximately twelve fifty-five this morning, a neighbor of yours, a spinster named Edith Baxter, heard shots. Do you happen to know her?"

"I do not."

"What was I thinking?" Cramer said, slapping his forehead.

"Of course you wouldn't know her. You've only lived here since New York was a small Dutch village, but I doubt if you could name a single neighbor other than your own Doctor Vollmer, since you almost never step outside. Anyway, Miss Baxter—the woman made very sure we knew she was a *miss*—said she heard two gunshots in the street and went to her bedroom window. She says a car screeched away—I'm using her word, *screeched*—and she saw a man prone on the sidewalk."

"Fascinating," Wolfe said, steepling his hands.

"Yeah, isn't it? And wait—it gets even more fascinating. Miss Baxter said the man on the sidewalk, who was wearing a suit and hat, got up as the car drove away and went into one of the houses along the block. This house, so she says. And from her description of the man, it could very well have been Goodwin here."

Wolfe turned to me. "Archie, do you have a comment?"

I knew what he wanted me to say. "Yes, sir, Mr. Cramer is correct. That was me, all right. I was walking home from my weekly poker game at Saul's when somebody in a car fired a couple of shots and then drove away fast. As the woman correctly stated, I dropped down onto the sidewalk. I was about to tell you about it when the inspector arrived."

"Do you believe you were the target of the shots?" Wolfe asked.

"I can't think why. It was probably some drunken kids out tearing up on a beautiful night," I said.

Cramer scowled. "And you didn't think to report it?"

"There was nothing to report, Inspector. I couldn't identify the car, it all happened so fast. As your Miss Baxter so correctly reported, I was prone and in no position to see the license plate—if the car even had one. About all I can say is that it probably was a prewar Dodge or a Plymouth, and I'm not even positive about that—or even about its color."

"And I suppose you both are going to tell me this had nothing to do with a case you're working on?" Cramer said.

"I have no commissions at the present time, nor have I had any recently," Wolfe said. "I am curious as to why you are investigating this, sir. There has been no homicide."

"As you very well know, we also investigate attempted homicides, and from where I'm sitting, this sure as my Aunt Betsy looks like an attempt on Goodwin. By the way, you may be interested to know that both slugs were recovered from the outside wall of one of your neighboring brownstones, the one just to the east. Thirty-two caliber, both of them, and they were embedded in the stone about eight feet above the sidewalk. Whoever fired was a lousy shot."

"Assuming the target really was Mr. Goodwin," Wolfe put in.

"Yeah, and until I learn differently, I'm going to stay with that assumption, thank you very much," Cramer said, gesturing toward me with his gnawed stogie. "This is not exactly a block where gunfire is common. The main thing that differentiates it from lots of similar blocks in this part of town is that you just happen to live here. And I'm not a great believer in coincidences."

"Nor am I, sir," Wolfe replied. "Although this occurrence may be one."

"Nuts. And I suppose that you're going to stick with your story that you're not working on anything right now?"

"It is not a story, sir, it is a fact. I have not undertaken a case in weeks, and I have no prospects for one at present."

Wolfe was telling the truth, as I knew only too well, since I maintain the checkbook, among my other duties. The current balance was at its lowest level in almost three years.

"As usual, I find myself wasting my time in this room," Cramer said with a snort, getting to his feet and jamming his battered fedora onto his head. "By God, I know I've said this before,

Wolfe, but it bears repeating: One of these days, you're going to get too clever for your own good. I know something's going on here, but getting information from you is like trying to wring blood out of a turnip." Having delivered his speech, the homicide inspector glared at each of us in turn and stormed down the hall to the front door, with me trailing in his wake and locking the door behind him.

CHAPTER 3

When I got back to the office, I found Wolfe in a somber mood, and I was feeling pretty somber myself. "We've made a lot of enemies over the years," I remarked as I dropped into my desk chair.

"Did you recognize the voice on the telephone?" he asked.

"No, but then it probably was disguised, with that high pitch and all."

"Perhaps. Do you have any thoughts?"

"I'm reminded of something you have said several times over the years: 'If someone has decided to kill you, and he is possessed of ordinary intelligence, you will die,' or words to that effect."

"There are always exceptions," Wolfe said, but his tone lacked conviction.

"In this case, I am all for exceptions. Where do we go from here?"

Wolfe drew in a bushel of air and let it out slowly. "Whenever you leave this house—and ventures out should be severely limited for now—you must use the rear exit." He was referring to a narrow passageway behind the brownstone that goes between a warehouse and an auto repair shop and leads out to Thirty-Fourth Street. At our end of the path, there is a solid wood gate seven feet high that has no knob or latch on the outside, only a Hotchkiss lock. But if someone is expected and knocks on the gate, it can be opened from the kitchen with the push of a button.

"So now I learn that I am under a form of house arrest. That's hardly an action plan, is it?"

"We find ourselves at war," Wolfe declared. "It is incumbent upon me to act, as I am the cause of these straits."

"A quibble," I said, using one of his favorite words. "At the risk of appearing self-important, I have done my share to alienate a variety of people in past investigations of ours. It is possible we may be dealing with someone who is holding a grudge against me, not you."

"I think it unlikely, but I am not about to debate the point, Archie. We have work to do."

"As in . . . ?"

"As in reviewing all of our cases over the last two decades. Anything older would no doubt be fruitless."

Wolfe and I differ in almost every way but one: we both take pride in being well-organized. One result is that we have amassed highly detailed records on each case we have tackled since I began drawing paychecks in the old brownstone. These records are stored by year in three locked four-drawer walnut filing cabinets in one corner of the office, each case given its own folder. We were about to undertake a trip down memory lane.

We spent all of the next two days wading through the files, and I use the first-person plural pronoun to be accurate. In what for him was a shocking departure, Wolfe chose to forgo his twice-daily visits to the plant rooms on the roof, which no doubt drove Theodore Horstmann, our orchid nurse, to the verge of a nervous breakdown. Even though old Horstmann is fully capable of coddling the ten thousand orchids himself, he remains convinced that without Wolfe's presence, those exotic specimens would somehow wither and die of neglect.

Back to our search through the archives. We each tackled one case at a time, and upon finishing it, we passed it to the other for review. Overall, I was surprised at how few people we seemed to have alienated, other than those, of course, who ended up going to prison or to that well-known electric chair up at Sing Sing on the Hudson.

It was those who got sent to the penitentiary, or their relatives, on whom we concentrated. "Regardless of the surety of a person's guilt," Wolfe said, "that malfeasant or his friends and relatives will focus their hatred upon me, and by extension upon you."

"Is that enough to drive someone to threaten murder?" I posed.

Wolfe lifted his shoulders and let them drop. "Who is to say? I knew of a man years ago in Romania who shot and killed a neighbor for no other reason than because the man had complained to local police about noisy parties at the neighbor's house."

"Okay, I will concede there are some nutcases out there like your trigger-happy Romanian, but so far, we haven't come across anybody who seems like the type to blast away at me."

"I do not concur, Archie. As we have gone over these cases, I have come up with five, or possibly six—"

He was cut short by the telephone, which I answered. "Nero Wolfe's office, Archie Goodwin speaking."

"Yes, Mr. Goodwin, you may recognize my voice." I gestured to Wolfe to pick up his receiver.

"It's possible I have heard it before," I said, gripping the phone.

"Of course you have, very recently, and I assume Nero Wolfe is on the line now, as well."

"I am," Wolfe snapped.

A mirthless chuckle. "Good, very good. If I know anything about human nature, the two of you probably have been searching your memories, and very possibly your records as well, these last two days, to see if you can figure out just who might want to kill Mr. Goodwin. Having any luck, boys?" Another chuckle, as dry as a saltine cracker.

"The reason for your call?" Wolfe asked.

"Just checking in to monitor your progress. And do not bother trying to trace this, assuming you have the technology. It is from a pay phone somewhere in our great city, and I am about to sign off. Good day to you both." The line went dead.

"Human nature, huh?" I said. "Nervy bastard."

"Nervy, maybe; insolent, without question—but a bastard? I do not possess the information with which to make such a judgment."

"Okay, you are the grammarian here, as you have pointed out to me so many times. You were making a point when we were so rudely interrupted."

"I was about to say that after having reviewed the files of our past commissions, I identified five or possibly six individuals whose enmity toward us is such that they might wish one or both of us dead. I have since revised that number to five."

"So, I am to hunt down all these people and shoot them before one gets me, right?"

"Stop prattling, Archie."

"I'm sorry, sir. It's a bad habit that I fall into—prattling, I mean—when I learn that someone wants to kill me."

Wolfe glowered at me. "When you have finished indulging

yourself by wallowing in self-pity, let us consider the list I have drawn up."

"The wallowing is over," I said, flipping open my notebook and swiveling to face him.

"Good. The names are Simeon Marx, Tobias Lester, Charles Stinson, Grover Applegate, and Bradley Jameson. Here are the files, to refresh your memory," he said, putting them on the corner of his desk within my reach.

"I recognize all of those monikers, of course," I said as I scooped up the folders, "although I'm sure you would claim this is only because I have also just been through the files myself, and at least three of them jumped out as possibilities to me, as well. I suppose you're testing me to see if I can figure out just why you fastened on this bunch."

"Your supposition is correct," Wolfe said, leaning back in his chair and closing his eyes. He was being smug, which made me determined to come up with some answers.

"Simeon Marx strangled that ballet dancer a dozen or so years back. Marx was a higher-up in one of the big Wall Street brokerage houses, and the ballerina was blackmailing him by threatening to tell his wife about their relationship. The cops were sure they had another man fingered for the killing, but the dancer's wealthy father—from down in Virginia—hired you to dig deeper, and you did."

"Just so." The folds in Wolfe's cheeks deepened, which for him is a smile.

"Simeon Marx ended up going to the chair, and his brother Alan loudly insisted he was innocent, that he was framed. If my memory holds, Alan Marx called you a number of names, including several that no newspaper will print."

"Your memory holds," Wolfe muttered. "Continue."

"Tobias Lester was known to his friends and in the society pages as Toby. And in said pages, either 'playboy' or 'man-about-town' invariably preceded his name. Almost nine years ago, Lester was one of a group of socialites partying on a yacht up north of the George Washington Bridge on the Hudson when a man fell overboard and drowned.

"The death was ruled an accident originally. However, one member of the group claimed she saw someone push the man, David Warren, but couldn't identify him in the darkness. The Warren family hired you to investigate, and you—with my intrepid legwork, I hasten to add—were able to make a strong case that Toby Lester was responsible for the killing because the dead man had won the affections of a young woman Lester thought of as his private property, so to speak.

"He was awaiting trial in the Tombs when he hanged himself with rope that somehow got smuggled in. Lester's sister, Maybelle, then held a press conference saying that her brother would have been cleared at a trial, and she claimed that you and I were directly responsible for his death. The only reason her claim about us didn't get more press was because of the prison system's high-profile—and unsuccessful—investigation into how Toby Lester was able to get ahold of the rope he used to kill himself. Have I left anything out?"

"Nothing of significance," Wolfe said, "other than to underscore my absolute certainty that Mr. Lester was the murderer, despite his sister's loud and offensive protestations."

"So noted. Next, we have Charles Stinson, a reclusive bachelor in his thirties who worked in a stamp and coin shop on East Twenty-Third Street and lived with his widowed mother near Stuyvesant Square. He was one of a half-dozen suspects in the bludgeoning death of a young woman on a promenade along the East River eleven years back.

"The police were getting nowhere—apparently the woman had been promiscuous, to say the least," I said. "Her rich—make that *very* rich—uncle, frustrated by the lack of progress on the part of Cramer and his crew, turned to us. Or rather, to you."

"When they hire me, they hire you," Wolfe put in after taking a healthy drink from the first of two beers Fritz had just brought in on a tray with a chilled pilsner glass.

"Anyway, you nailed the creep, who finally broke down in tears right here in the office. A pathetic sight, a pathetic little man. As far as I'm aware, he is still up in Attica and will be for the rest of his days.

"Somehow, his mouthpiece, a lowly public defender no less, gave such an impassioned defense of Stinson's mental state that he got him off with life rather than the chair. His mother, Anna, despite her son's confession, could not believe her dear boy had done something so awful, and at least two of the local dailies quoted her as calling you an 'ogre' and a 'charlatan,' among other names."

"Don't forget 'mountebank.' I rather liked that one," Wolfe said.

"I guess I'd forgotten. What does it mean?"

"A huckster, a hawker of quack medicines, an out-and-out phony."

"At least Anna Stinson has a big vocabulary. Next, we move on to Grover Applegate. This one was not a murderer," I said.

"No, but he *was* a miscreant of the first rank."

"Yeah, he'll have a hard time passing through the Pearly Gates, all right," I said as I opened his folder and scanned the report. "He was a well-known financial adviser who handled the money of a lot of rich old ladies. I remember him well. He conned them out of millions until little Mrs. Ferguson came to you on the advice of a former client of yours, Melville Perkins, whom you had helped get rid of a sleazy blackmailer.

"She was a neighbor of Perkins in one of those tony co-ops up on Park Avenue, and she thought something was funny, and confusing, about the way Applegate was moving her dough around."

"Moving much of it into his own accounts," Wolfe remarked.

"After you exposed him, Applegate went to prison, and he died there two years later of a heart attack. His son, Grover Jr., who thought from the beginning that dear old dad was innocent of all wrongdoing, claimed publicly that you killed him just as surely as if you had put a bullet through his heart."

"The young man was given to hyperbole," Wolfe said.

"He also said you would roast in the fires of hell. More hyperbole, I guess. Anyway, I think it's safe to say that we can definitely count the younger Applegate as an enemy.

"Now we go to the last person on your list, one Bradley Jameson. I remember that case like it was yesterday, no need for me to look at the file or have you prompt me. With a name like his, it seems like he should have been a banker or a company president instead of a hockey player—and not just any player, but an all-star goalie for the Rangers.

"There had been a brawl in a saloon on Second Avenue several years back. A graduate student at Columbia got a fractured skull in the melee and fell into a coma. When the police tried to find out who hit the kid, they were met with a conspiracy of silence from everyone who'd been in the joint. The boy's father hired you to learn who did it, and you delivered."

"With your and Saul's help," Wolfe said.

"Particularly Saul's. He found out that the barkeep had served time for being the wheelman in an armed robbery up in Utica some years earlier. That's a felony, and felons cannot hold a liquor license in this state. You had the bar owner over a barrel, so to speak. He had a choice: tell you who mauled the young man or lose his profitable watering hole.

"So he sang, and the words he came up with were . . . *Bradley Jameson*. No wonder everybody in that bar had clammed up. Hockey's regular season had just ended, and the playoffs were about to begin. For once, the Rangers were favored to win the Stanley Cup, but after you presented Jameson to the police, everything changed. Normally, in a case like that, there would have been continuances—allowing Jameson to play—but this brawl happened just after another man had been killed in a bar fight, and the district attorney was under pressure from the mayor and the newspapers, so bail was denied. Have I left anything out?"

"Not so far," Wolfe said.

"The star goalie quickly went to trial and was found guilty of assault and battery, and attempted murder, and got sent to stir. In the meantime, the substitute goalie was a sieve, and Detroit ran up some big scores against the Rangers on their way to winning the Cup. One sports columnist wrote that you were 'the most hated man in New York,' with the D.A. right behind you on the hate list."

"More hyperbole."

"I suppose, but you did get several pieces of hate mail, including a few that suggested the world would be better off without you."

"I discount the ranting of zealots," Wolfe said.

"I have been to enough Rangers games at the Garden to realize many of the seats are filled with those you term 'zealots.' And having seen these people in action, I would not be quick to discount them."

Wolfe reacted with a shrug. "It was Mr. Jameson whom I found to be of the greatest concern. He forcefully suggested at the time of his sentencing that I had not heard the last of him."

"I haven't kept track, but he's probably out of the cooler by now. Luckily for him, the Columbia student recovered, so the charge wasn't upgraded to murder or manslaughter. Now that we have reviewed the five cases you selected, I have a number of questions."

"I will try to mask my surprise."

"Did I detect just a touch of sarcasm? I will ignore it and plow on: First, two of the people angriest with you are women—Maybelle Lester and Anna Stinson. Yet the voice from the two phone calls seemed to be that of a man, albeit disguised. Do you feel that lets the ladies off the hook?"

"Not necessarily, and you should know that, as an expert on women and their foibles," Wolfe said. "Either of them could easily have enlisted a consort to speak for her. Many, if not most, women are adept at getting men to do their bidding. It also is likely that if one of the females were the instigator of the calls, she may have felt a male voice would be more threatening and intimidating."

"Okay, I'll give you that one," I said, grinning and throwing up my hands in mock surrender. "How do you explain that all of these events happened five or more years ago—a couple of them more than a decade back—yet someone waited until now to exact revenge?"

"Revenge may be sweetest when contemplated over an extended period," Wolfe replied.

"Nice. Who said that—Shakespeare?"

"I did. I once knew a man who waited more than twenty years before killing the cousin who had assaulted his wife. And at least once a year in each of those two decades, he reminded the cousin, sometimes in subtle ways, that he knew of his transgression."

"You are filled with stories, a few of them possibly even true. All right, we have identified some possible suspects who could be behind these calls. Where do we go from here?"

"We begin by inviting Saul to dinner tonight. Call him and tell him we are having a casserole of lamb cutlets with gammon and potatoes. I recall that he enjoyed those cutlets on a previous occasion. And have him arrive through the passageway in the rear."

We, indeed, were under siege.

CHAPTER 4

Saul Panzer is one of the handful of people Wolfe invites to dine with us in the old brownstone. Among the others are Orrie Cather, an operative we frequently use; Lon Cohen of the *Gazette*; the wealthy Long Island orchid-grower Lewis Hewitt; our physician and neighbor, Doc Vollmer; our lawyer, Nathaniel Parker; and on rare occasions, Inspector Cramer, who will put aside any animosities toward Wolfe and me for the pleasure of sampling the culinary miracles wrought by Fritz Brenner. Fred Durkin, another operative Wolfe employs almost as often as Saul, has had numerous meals in the house over the years also, but because he has committed such sins as putting vinegar on food before tasting it, he has been relegated to eating in the kitchen with Fritz.

At ten minutes to seven, the back doorbell rang, and I let our dinner guest into the kitchen. Saul Panzer would not impress you with his appearance. He stands about five foot seven and tips the scales at one hundred and forty pounds, give or take a few ounces. His long face is dominated by an oversize nose, and he always seems to be in need of a shave. His shoulders are stooped and his dust-colored hair usually needs combing, although on this night, he had it slicked down in deference to the occasion and had left his battered brown cap at home. He also had donned a suit, white shirt, and tie—another concession to the evening.

But you should not for a moment let Saul's looks deceive you. He happens to be the best operative, freelance or otherwise, in New York's five boroughs, and probably in the whole of the country. He is next to invisible when on a tail, and no one can match him at ferreting out clues. He commands double the rates of most freelancers but never lacks for business, although he will drop anything else he is doing if Nero Wolfe needs him for a job.

The two men have great respect for each other, and Wolfe has said numerous times that he trusts Saul "more than thought credible," with which I concur. A bachelor, Saul lives on a spacious full floor of the building on East Thirty-Eighth Street that I referred to earlier. To keep him company, he has a grand piano; floor-to-ceiling shelves stocked with books he has read; museum-caliber art decorating the walls; and a well-stocked bar and wine cellar. His earnings over the years also have enabled him to buy three buildings in his old neighborhood in Brooklyn—buildings that each have shot up in value.

Stepping into the kitchen, Saul waved a "hello" to Fritz and gave me a "what's-going-on-with-this-backdoor-stuff?" look. My response was a "you'll-find-out-before-the-evening-is-over" grin.

Business talk is verboten at Wolfe's dinner table, and that night would be no exception. The conversation ranged from the economic shortcomings of the Soviet system to a comparison of the construction methods of Egyptian and Aztec pyramids and the advantages of each. Saul had some opinions; I mostly nodded and chewed. After dinner, followed by a dessert of strawberries Romanoff, we repaired to the office for coffee and then drinks.

Saul sat in the red leather chair with a snifter of cognac on the small table at his elbow, while Wolfe had beer and I sipped scotch.

"You, of course, wonder why you were asked to come via the passageway tonight," Wolfe said.

"I do. Although I know something is up, because I cased the street before I went around the back way, and parked at one end of your block, there's an unmarked car with a plainclothes man behind the wheel, trying without success to look inconspicuous. One of Cramer's minions, no doubt."

Wolfe raised his eyebrows. "I wasn't aware of that. Were you, Archie?"

"No, sir. Interesting."

"All right, it is time you received the full picture." For the next half hour, Wolfe proceeded to lay everything out, from the shots fired at me to the two threatening phone calls and our review of the case files.

"Lovin' babe!" Saul said after Wolfe had finished. That's the Panzer equivalent of swearing, and the strongest language I've ever heard him use.

"Indeed," Wolfe said. "Do you have any thoughts?"

"It seems like somebody has waited an awfully long time before taking revenge on you. Any possibility that it's someone other than the people connected to those five cases?"

"Of course it is possible," Wolfe replied, "but those are the episodes that have generated the most intense animosity toward me by far."

"I was at least peripherally involved in three . . . no, four of those cases, and I remember the anger," Saul said. "What can I be doing?"

Wolfe's mouth twitched. "I had hoped this would pique your interest. Can you make some inquiries—discreet ones, at least at first—about the living principals in those five files? We can bring on Fred, if you think it would help."

"I'll fly solo, at least for now," Saul said, turning to me. "Are you hunkering down here?"

"Too damned much of the time," I grumped. "I have snuck out—by the back way, of course—to take Lily Rowan to dinner and to transact some banking. Unfortunately, the latter activity has involved withdrawals lately, not deposits," I added, looking at Wolfe.

"Any idea if your phantom caller knows about that passageway to Thirty-Fourth Street?"

"I'm not sure, but I doubt it."

Saul nodded. "Because this rocky old island of ours is lacking in alleys, most people mistakenly think the only way in and out of a building is through the street entrance."

"The paucity of alleyways in this city can be traced to an egregious decision made generations ago by so-called municipal planners," Wolfe put in. "These men felt alleys would take up valuable space that could better be used for structures. The consequences of that act are all too apparent to anyone traversing New York's streets: refuse piled high on the sidewalks in front of commercial establishments and residences, and garbage and delivery trucks parked and double-parked in front of these same buildings, impeding vehicular and pedestrian traffic."

I was tempted to point out that because Wolfe rarely leaves the brownstone, he has little exposure to—and little reason to complain about—such unpleasant conditions as garbage and deliveries stacked up on so many Midtown sidewalks, but I was not about to debate the issue. Besides, our dinner guest had more to say about back entrances in Manhattan, and Wolfe loves to hear him talk.

"Over the years, I have come to discover all sorts of narrow passageways between buildings that lead away from presumably undetected rear exits," Saul said.

"Handy for burglars to know," I remarked.

"You can say that again, Archie. Case in point: A dozen or so years back, I got hired by a rag trade nabob who owned a duplex in a six-story building in the Village—a dandy setup. His wife's jewels—a haul worth close to a half million—had been pilfered from an upstairs bedroom, or at least the most valuable ones had, the diamonds and rubies. The cops were stumped. There were doormen on duty around the clock, and they said they never admitted any strangers to the building, which I believed. However, the place had a rear exit that opened on a narrow, winding passage between two buildings that ended at MacDougal Street.

"The lock on the rear exit to the duplex was intact, which means it had been picked," Saul continued. "That smelled like Eddie 'Light Fingers' Cornelius, who could work wonders with locks and who also was known for his skill at lifting expensive baubles. To make a long story short, I ran Eddie to ground before he could fence the stuff and gave him a choice: give me the diamonds and rubies or get turned over to the law."

"Let me guess," I said. "Eddie coughed up the gems, you didn't tell the cops, and you returned the ice to its owner like the noble fellow you are."

"Bingo! But there's more to the story that will interest both of you. I also got Eddie to give me a dandy fold-out map he had, although he didn't like it one bit. He had put this map together himself, or so he claimed, and he did a good job. It covered Manhattan, river to river and from the Village on the south to Ninetieth Street on the north. It showed dozens of passageways between buildings that he had inked in. Very helpful for anyone wanting access to the rear of a structure."

"Like maybe a jewel thief," I observed. Saul grinned and took another sip of cognac.

"Most interesting," Wolfe said. "But it begs a question."

"The answer is no," Saul replied.

I spun around in my chair. "What question? What did I miss here?"

Wolfe made a sound like a chuckle. "I wondered whether that map showed our own path from the back door to Thirty-Fourth Street, and Saul told me what I wanted to hear."

"Hell, I could have told you so," I said, trying to recover from being flummoxed. "Like it or not, we are not exactly in a high-rent district here. Nowhere near in a league with Park Avenue or the Upper East Side, or even certain parts of Greenwich Village. This Eddie character apparently knows where the pickings are best."

"I will give him that," Saul said. "He's one slimy character, but he's also damned shrewd."

"Do we really care that our own back exit isn't on his map?" I posed.

Saul nodded. "I think you should care and be thankful, Archie. Guys like Eddie, who are smart enough to come up with a map like he did, also know how valuable it can be to others who want to, shall we say, stay out of sight as much as possible. I'm under no illusion that the map I have is Eddie's only copy. I would not be surprised to learn that he's made copies of it and peddled them at a nice price to all sorts of people who prefer not to be seen on the streets."

"I agree with your assumption," Wolfe said, draining the last of his second post-dinner beer.

"Thank you, sir, and thank you also for the superb dinner," Saul said. "Please convey my thanks to Fritz for another memorable gastronomic experience. Do you prefer that I leave the way I came?"

"I do. For now, let us maintain the fiction that we are an armed camp, letting no one in or out. We must remain vigilant. As Winston Churchill once said, 'We shall defend our island, whatever the cost may be.'"

After Saul left and I bolted the back door, I poured myself a glass of milk in the kitchen and returned to the office, dropping into my desk chair. "Do you feel safer knowing that an unmarked car occupied by one of New York's Finest sits at the end of the block, presumably protecting us from the forces of evil?" I asked.

Wolfe's reply was a scowl.

"I feel the same way," I told him. "But I will sleep well regardless. I have no doubt that our fortifications will keep the barbarians at bay."

That earned me another scowl, which I returned with a grin as I rose to go upstairs to bed. It had been a long day.

CHAPTER 5

After putting away a breakfast of broiled Georgia ham and hash brown potatoes in the kitchen, I complimented Fritz on the ham and went to the office, where I glared at the telephone on my desk, wondering when we would get another call from the man—I continued to believe it was a man—with the high-pitched voice. As if it could read my mind, the instrument rang at that very moment.

I recited the usual "Nero Wolfe's office, Archie Goodwin speaking," and held my breath.

"Oh yes, Mr. Goodwin, I know that you work with Mr. Wolfe." It was a woman's voice, with no regional accent. "You sound most pleasant," she added.

"I am told my phone manners are one of my strongest suits, Miss—or is it Mrs. . . . ?"

"It's Miss—Miss Cordelia Hutchinson."

"A very nice name. What can we do for you?"

"I would like to . . . well, to hire your Mr. Nero Wolfe," she said, her voice now just above a whisper, as if someone were listening.

"Are you alone?"

"Yes, yes I am, quite alone." Still near a whisper.

"Then feel free to speak a little louder, Miss Hutchinson. Tell me why you want to hire Mr. Wolfe."

"It is very personal," she confided. "Terribly personal."

"I assure you that's normally the case when people seek Mr. Wolfe's assistance. But I will need more specifics about your concerns before I talk to him. As I am sure you can appreciate, he is a very busy man."

"Oh, I am sure that he is, Mr. Goodwin, I am sure that he is. I have read much about his reputation. But won't he accept me as a client if I say to you that my situation is very . . . well, very frightening?"

"I can ask him, of course, but I am being candid when I say that unless he knows more about your situation, he is not likely to see you."

There was a long pause on the other end. I thought I might have lost her except that I could hear breathing.

"All right," she sighed after a half-minute, which seemed longer. "Please tell Mr. Wolfe I am being blackmailed, and it is destroying my life."

"Can you give me any more information about this blackmailing? As in: Who is doing it, and why? Take your time."

"I do not think you realize how hard this is for me, Mr. Goodwin," she said, her voice starting to crack. "I have thought about making this call now for almost a week. I am glad you can't see me at this moment, because my hands are shaking."

"You do realize, Miss Hutchinson, that if Mr. Wolfe does agree to see you, and that is by no means certain, he will ask you the same questions I am going to, and many, many more, some of them very direct and demanding of answers."

"Yes . . . I understand that."

"How did you hear from the blackmailer?"

"Letters, two of them, and a telephone call."

"I assume you live in New York City?"

"I do now, yes. Up on Sutton Place, with my parents."

"Where can I reach you?"

"I would prefer calling you again."

"Have it your way. Because you seem to know something about Nero Wolfe, you are probably aware that he does not come cheap."

"Money is not an issue for me, Mr. Goodwin."

"All right, Miss Hutchinson. I will discuss your case, such as I know of it, with Mr. Wolfe today. I suggest you telephone me sometime after four this afternoon, and I will tell you his decision."

"That is so very kind, thank you. You sound like a nice person. Please tell him that I am desperate." Her voice began to crack again.

"I will tell him. I expect to hear from you shortly after four." She promised she would call, and we signed off.

I then dialed the direct line of Lon Cohen of the *New York Gazette,* who I mentioned earlier. Lon is not only a good poker player, he is a newspaperman extraordinaire, and we have tapped his knowledge of the city and its inhabitants more times than I can count. But in return, he has gotten a bundle of scoops on cases Wolfe has solved. Lon does not have a title I am aware of at the *Gazette*, America's fifth-largest daily newspaper, but he does have an office on the twentieth floor of the paper's Midtown tower, just two doors from the publisher himself.

He answered on the first ring. "Tidings of the day, oh chronicler of the foibles and follies of the daily life in our nation's greatest city," I said.

"Calling to chortle because of your winnings with the pasteboards the other night?" he snapped.

"Heaven forbid that I should ever chortle. Over the long haul, you have picked my pocket more times than I have picked yours on the green baize of Saul's poker table. I come before you, hat in hand, humbly seeking information."

"Huh! You've never done anything humbly in your life. Well, out with it, gumshoe. We do have deadlines here, you know."

"As you have so often reminded me. What can you tell me about one Cordelia Hutchinson?"

"The comely young railroad millionairess? What do you need to know? And why?"

"Whoa! One question at a time, scrivener. We may—and I do mean *may*—have us a client, but that is anything but certain right at the moment. And it is not for publication at this time."

"Understood. I can tell you a little about said young lady off the top of my head, although I'll call the morgue for the clips on her, if you'd like to take a look at them—but only in my office, of course."

A half hour later, after leaving the brownstone by the rear exit, I was in Lon's small, unadorned office with a dandy view of the Chrysler Building, listening to him chew out an editor in the newsroom fifteen floors below over the phone.

"What do you mean, our man on the Capitol beat doesn't know how to reach the congressman? Whatever happened to enterprise reporting, for God's sake? The guy is clearly holed up someplace and doesn't want to talk about that lady he's been seen with all over Washington. Where in the hell are our reporter's contacts? Damn, if the *Times* or the *Herald-Tribune* or, heaven forbid, the *Daily News,* beats us to this, there will be hell to pay, and several people on this paper will be doing the paying—and that includes you."

Lon slammed the receiver down so hard I thought it would break. "Pretty impressive," I told him. "Are you always that hard to please?"

"Archie, you haven't seen anything. Two weeks ago, I had a guy canned because of—oh, never mind, it's not worth retelling. Okay, here are the Hutchinson clips." He slid two fat envelopes across the desk to me.

"Your crew has written quite a bit about her," I said.

"Almost all of it in the society pages, which I know you do not usually read. Am I sniffing a scandal someplace here?"

"Is the lady someone who might be part of a scandal?" I countered.

Lon ran his hand over dark, slicked-back hair. "Beats me, Archie. She's young, single, twenty-four or so, nice-looking but just short of beautiful, or so I would say. You can look at the pictures of her and judge for yourself. The last few years, she's been linked with a number of eligible swells, most of them who come from money like her."

I went through the clippings and agreed with Lon's assessment of Cordelia: Her photos showed her to be fresh-faced, well turned-out, and undeniably pretty—but beautiful? Not quite. An article several years old focused on her coming-out party on the rolling green of the family's splendid estate up near Katonah. Other stories, some with pictures, placed her at elegant gatherings in Newport and the Hamptons, always smiling demurely and clad in elegant designer gowns.

The three most recent articles, all from the last six months, included pictures of Cordelia with Lance "Lanny" Mercer III, heir to the Mercer Aviation Corp. millions. Perhaps the respective families were hoping for a dynastic marriage to merge their rail and aeronautic empires.

All the while I was going through the *Gazette*'s material on Miss Hutchinson, Lon was on one or another of his three phones firing off orders like a drill sergeant addressing a bunch of raw recruits. "Always instructive to see you in action," I told him, rising to leave. "Thanks for getting me the clips."

"Just remember the favor," he muttered, waving a hand absently and preparing to make another call. I pitied whoever would be its recipient.

I was back in the office transferring orchid germination records onto file cards at eleven when Wolfe came down from the plant rooms, placed a raceme of *Cattleya* in the vase on his desk blotter, asked if I had slept well, and buzzed Fritz in the kitchen for beer.

"I scanned the block from my bedroom window this morning, and it appears the police car is gone," I told him when he had gotten his bulk settled and begun riffling through the morning mail I had opened and stacked on the desk.

"No doubt Inspector Cramer has lost interest in the foofaraw of the other night. He has plenty of larger day-to-day worries."

"No doubt. By the way, we got a telephone call this morning."

"From . . . *that* man?"

"No, from—believe it or not—a prospective client."

"Pah! I am not interested. You know that."

"*Pah*, yourself. You are well aware of the sorry state of our bank balance. This is the answer to our prayers."

"Yours, perhaps, but not mine," Wolfe said, popping the cap on the first of two chilled bottles of beer Fritz had placed before him. "Besides, we have other matters to deal with."

"Which is precisely what Saul is doing. We can't let this bird knock us out of commission—and commissions. As you have so often said in this very room, it takes a lot of money to run the operation here, what with salaries for Fritz, Theodore, and me, to say nothing of the grocery bills, the books you buy by the dozen, and, of course, the beer."

"I do not buy books by the dozen," Wolfe said with a sniff.

"Okay, so I threw that in just to see if you were listening. But over the course of a year, you do help to keep our local bookseller, Mr. Murger, in the black. I've been getting rusty sitting around, and I need some action or I will start to get cranky. You surely don't want that to happen."

Wolfe raised his eyebrows. "*Start* to get cranky? I was not aware you had ever ceased."

"Do you see what I mean? When we don't have business, we get on each other's nerves. I know you hate to hear this, but we need to be working, and not just for the money, although it helps."

I was getting to him. He began tracing circles with his index finger on the arm of his chair and drew in his usual cubic bushel of air. Letting it out, he conceded, "All right, who was the caller?" I stifled a smile and mentioned her name.

"The railway heiress, I believe," Wolfe said.

"So you read the society columns, eh?"

"On occasion. Report."

I gave him a verbatim account of my conversation with Cordelia Hutchinson—hardly challenging given its brevity—and summarized my findings in the *Gazette*'s files on the young lady. As I talked, Wolfe's facial expressions varied from unease to outright disgust. When I finished, he leaned back, eyes closed, and laced his hands over his stomach.

After a prolonged sigh, he stirred. "Confound it, have her come."

"When?"

"Tomorrow morning, eleven."

"Should I have her arrive through the passageway?"

"Yes, give her the directions. If she asks you why, tell her it is to protect her privacy."

"She'll buy that. Do I have any other instructions in the meantime?"

"Find out if Saul has made any progress on his assignments and ask Miss Rowan her opinion of Miss Hutchinson. I presume their paths have crossed in the world of what the newspapers term 'high society.'"

I mentioned Lily Rowan earlier. She and I have been what might be called "special friends" for years, and I see no need to elaborate on that term. Lily is very beautiful, very lazy, and very rich. Her wealth comes from her late father, an Irish immigrant who made a fortune building much of New York City's current sewer system.

Although Nero Wolfe has an aversion to women, he long ago made an exception for Lily, at least in part because the first time they met, she asked, demurely, if she might be allowed to see his vast array of orchids in the greenhouse. This is a request Wolfe rarely rejects, as his pride in his orchids is every bit as great as his love of fine foods and good books.

Lily lives in a penthouse topping a ten-story building just off Park Avenue that contains, among other things, an off-white Austrian grand piano with ninety-seven keys; artworks by Renoir, Monet, Picasso, and Matisse; and a nineteen-by-thirty-four–foot Kashan carpet in seven colors. I have said that Lily is lazy, but I must also mention that she has a strong social conscience and generously lends both her time and her money to several "good works" organizations that aid the less fortunate. One more point: Lily's wealth is not what attracted me to her, and whenever we venture out, whether to dinner, the theatre, or a hockey game at the Garden, I pay—period.

"To what do I owe this call, Escamillo?" Lily asked, using the name she tagged me with after I had had a run-in with a very angry bull in an Upstate meadow some years back.

"I seek information," I told her.

"Ah, I might have known! Is that all I am to you, a source of dirt on the great and the near-great in this sordid metropolis of ours?"

"You know better than that, fair lady. I cherish you for your grace on the dance floor, your winning smile, your wonderful sense of humor, your love of the New York Rangers—which I share—and, of course, your ability to cheer me up when I fall into a dark mood."

"You say the sweetest things to a girl. I trust you are not now in one of those dark moods."

"No, but if I were, the sound of your voice would have lifted me out of it already. What I would like today is any knowledge you have of one Miss Hutchinson of the railroad dynasty."

"The fetching Cordelia? Isn't she just a bit young for you?"

"Age knows no barriers, where love is concerned."

"Beautifully said, you sweet-talker. Now why do you really want to know about her?"

"You've seen right through me, as usual. Believe it or not, she may just become a client of ours."

"That is indeed hard to believe. Cordelia and I don't know each other well, but we did serve together on the board of an orphanage last year. I was rotating off the board as she was joining it, so we overlapped for a few months. I found her to be reserved and humble to the point of meekness, which I suspect is an affectation. If I had to use one word to describe her, it would be *prissy*."

"Any gossip floating around about said maiden?"

"Not that I have heard, although I probably wouldn't hear it, given that we run in different circles. I do know that she's been spending a lot of time with a young man from a family that builds airplanes."

"The Mercers."

"It sounds like you've done some homework of your own."

"A little. Just enough to know that I don't know very much about Cordelia Hutchinson."

"Of course, I am dying to know why she needs the services of Nero Wolfe and his noble associate Archie Goodwin. But I don't suppose you are going to tell me now, are you?"

"Not at the moment, but perhaps when this all gets resolved, I may share some details with you—that is, if you are nice to me."

"When have I not been nice to you, Escamillo?"

"Point taken. I have no complaints whatever about your behavior toward me. And I do like the sound of 'noble associate.'"

"I am certainly glad to hear that. But beware of Cordelia. She may just try to beguile you with her coy ways."

"Heaven forbid that you should think such a thing. After all, she's practically a child."

"Just remember, someone once said that age knows no barriers where love is concerned."

I promised her I would keep that in mind.

CHAPTER 6

At two minutes after four that afternoon, the phone rang in the office. Answering as I usually do, I was greeted by Cordelia Hutchinson's breathless voice. "Oh, Mr. Goodwin, have you talked to Mr. Wolfe?" I told her I had.

"Will he, will he . . . take me on?"

"That remains to be seen, Miss Hutchinson, but he will see you, which is progress of a sort. To protect your privacy, you are to come here via the back way," I said, explaining that I would meet her on Thirty-Fourth Street in front of the auto repair shop.

"What should I do to persuade him to take me on as a client? I'll do anything you say."

"First, be prompt. Eleven means eleven, so be on Thirty-Fourth Street no later than ten-fifty. Answer all of his questions, fully and honestly. Do not, under any circumstances, get cute. He is very direct—some would say curt—very straightforward, and he does not appreciate people who try to flatter him. Anything else you want to know?"

"No . . . I guess not. Will you be present when I talk to him?"

"Yes, but it is his show all the way. I'm just there as an observer."

"I am so glad that you will be there, though, Mr. Goodwin," she said in a faux little-girl voice that was beginning to get on my nerves. "You sound like you're a very nice man."

I was tempted to tell her not to try flattering me, either, but I let her comment slide. No sense giving her a hard time; she would get enough of that from Wolfe.

In the office the next morning, I finished typing letters Wolfe had dictated the day before to three orchid growers and put them on his desk blotter for signing. Then I called Saul for an update.

"Slow going, Archie," he said, "really slow. I feel like I'm taking Mr. Wolfe's money under false pretenses—that is, if I even charge him for my time on this one. So far, I haven't been able to eliminate anybody."

"We'll worry about that later. Fill me in."

"I started out with the case of Charles Stinson, the guy who went to prison for killing that young woman down along the East River."

"The man whose mother ripped into us for daring to suggest her angel was capable of such a horrible deed," I said.

"Right, and from my visits with her neighbors, it seems that the woman remains absolutely convinced of her son's innocence."

"Have you talked to her?"

"Not yet," Saul said. "Remember, Mr. Wolfe told me to make discreet inquiries. It seems Mrs. Stinson is not popular in her building or on the block. She has a mean temper, and often screams from her window at kids playing stickball on the sidewalk or in the street. She refuses to speak to most of her neighbors because of real or imagined slights, so I was told by several people."

"Other than her son, has she got any relatives?"

"None. Her husband died about twenty years ago, and her son was an only child. The only mail she ever gets is bills or circulars—no cards or letters."

"People certainly like to know one another's business, don't they?"

Saul agreed. "I wasn't even asked by any of these neighbors why I was interested in Anna Stinson. They were only too happy to volunteer their opinions about her, all of them negative. I had trouble leaving one woman's flat; she wanted to tell me all about Mrs. S., as well as some of the other people in the building and why she couldn't stand any of them."

"Well, you sound none the worse for the experience, trying as it must have been. Do we know anything about how Charles Stinson is faring?"

"He's still residing at Attica, of course. I just happen to know a guy fairly high up in the state penal system—I did a favor for him once—and he checked on Stinson for me. He's apparently as reclusive as ever, keeps to himself, has no friends whatsoever on the inside, and seems to like it that way. He has been in and out of the psychiatric ward and suffers from depression. Barely speaks."

"It seems unlikely he would enlist somebody to threaten us," I observed.

"*Unlikely* isn't a strong enough word," Saul said. "I would use *impossible*."

"So we scratch Charles Stinson off, but definitely not his mother. Who, or what, is next?"

"Alan Marx, the brother of Simeon, the stockbroker who strangled the blackmailing ballet dancer."

"Another vocal member of the Nero Wolfe fan club."

"This one's a hard man to pin down, Archie. Like his brother, Alan has worked on Wall Street and, by all accounts, has been successful. He's also a fine-art collector of note and a patron of all sorts of other arts, including opera, ballet, symphony, you name it. I did locate one broker who used to work with him and is with a different firm now. He told me that Alan Marx is a vindictive man who never forgets a slight, however minor. And I didn't have any trouble getting the former coworker to open up on the subject. Unprompted, he even brought up Alan's animosity toward Mr. Wolfe, which he said surfaced frequently when they had worked together."

"It doesn't sound like your source and Marx were exactly chummy."

"No, and if I were to guess, I would venture that my source left Alan Marx's brokerage house because of some sort of disagreement between them. When I pressed him on the subject, he clammed up."

"It doesn't appear we can cross the angry brother off our list."

"Archie, based on what I've found, I would not cross anybody off yet, except Charles Stinson," Saul said somberly.

"But, of course, not his vituperative mother. So the knives are out for us. Who's next?"

"The Lester family, specifically Maybelle, sister of the late Toby, who hanged himself up in the Tombs. I managed to locate a former family maid, Helen Stark, who had worked for the Lester family until she got tired of Maybelle's bullying ways and quit to take a job with another well-heeled family on the Upper East Side a little less than a year ago. Miss Stark told me the Lester woman is every bit as bitter about her brother's fate as she was when he died. She told me she heard Maybelle mutter to herself about 'that damned miserable Nero Wolfe' a number of times."

"How often I've muttered those very same words myself," I said. "Do you consider this woman to be a reliable witness, given her less-than-pleasant history with the family?"

"I do, Archie. I say that partly because Helen Stark also had some sympathetic words for Maybelle. 'I always tried to be tolerant of that sad lady, because I know her life has not been easy,' Helen told me. 'Her late father always favored Toby, and then she got herself jilted just two weeks before the big wedding her family had planned for her up at St. John the Divine. That soured her on marriage, and I hope I do not sound unkind when I say that she is not overly attractive, so she may not get another chance, whether she wants it or not. Even though she was not always nice to me, I do not wish her ill in any way. She's had more than her share of misery, poor woman, despite her wealth. And she's never gotten over her brother's suicide.'"

"So Maybelle could still be gunning for us. . . . Make that *me*."

"Maybe," Saul replied. "She's certainly got the dough to hire a hit man, if that happens to be in her plans."

"You're certainly full of good news," I said. "Well, go ahead, depress me further. I can take it."

"Next, we come to Grover Applegate Jr., son of the man who fleeced little old ladies and died in prison of a heart attack."

"Ah, the 'swindler of the century,' or so the newspapers termed the father at the time."

"And to this day, the son insists his old man was innocent," Saul said.

"Just like Mrs. Stinson. Seems that nobody thinks those near and dear can possibly be possessed of evil. Have you talked to the son?"

"No, but through people I know in the financial world, I did get in touch with a man named Mark Whelan, who used to work with Junior at one of the big Wall Street banks. From what he said, the younger Applegate remains every bit as bitter as Maybelle Lester."

"My boss sure knows how to make friends for life," I said.

"I don't suppose the son works for the same banking house his father did?"

"No, and that may be at least part of his resentment. Whelan told me that when Junior tried to get a job there, the bank wouldn't have anything to do with him because of his name. The Applegate stigma was too much for them. Not only that, he was also turned away by several other banks, and he was convinced he was being blackballed because of his father."

"But he *did* finally land a job?"

"Yes, at a smaller banking house, according to Whelan," Saul said. "They hired young Applegate because they felt he showed promise and deserved a chance to emerge from his father's long shadow."

"I sense there's a *but* coming."

"There is, Archie. *But* Applegate's 'poor me' attitude was so all-consuming that it affected his performance. Several times, the higher-ups at the bank urged him to be more positive; his foul moods and grumbling about his father's fate were casting a gloom over the office and causing coworkers to complain about him. The bank finally decided to let him go—although Whelan told me he got a better severance deal than his short tenure there, less than a year, merited."

"So what is he doing now?" I asked.

"Whelan thinks he's selling insurance, which is hardly a way to get rich quick. I wouldn't worry too much about him from a financial standpoint, though. His wife comes from plenty of money, one of the big North Carolina tobacco companies. They have a co-op someplace on the Upper East Side that Whelan says was featured in a slick home decorating magazine once."

"Is the elder Applegate's wife alive?"

"I was about to bring that up. After her husband was found

guilty of all his swindling, she got shunned by her neighbors and friends—make that *former* friends. Fortunately, she was left with enough money to live on, but she left the Park Avenue digs they had lived in for many years and is now somewhere over in Jersey, trying to be as inconspicuous as possible. By the way, the fact she was ostracized is another reason her son is so bitter.

"One more thing," Saul said. "Whelan told me he just happened to run into Applegate in a bar on First Avenue a month or so ago, and the guy was pretty well lit. He was still complaining about Nero Wolfe, using an adjective I won't repeat."

"You don't have to. I get the picture."

"Anyway, he went on ranting about Wolfe until damned near everybody in the saloon was looking at him, and the bartender had to tell him to pipe down or get out."

"With that personality, it's a wonder he ever sells any insurance."

"Whelan is under the impression that he's not doing very well," Saul said. "Have you heard enough?"

I said I had, and he moved on to Bradley Jameson, the onetime Rangers goalie who had blamed Wolfe for prematurely ending his career. "He is one nasty piece of work," Saul pronounced. "I talked to a copy editor in the *Daily News* sports department who I grew up with in Brooklyn, and he tells me Jameson has been arrested three or four times over the last few years for public drunkenness and disturbing the peace. He slugged somebody in a bar fight and the guy ended up in the hospital with a broken nose. He came close to losing an eye."

"Does Jameson have a job?"

"He was working for a while as—believe it or not—a bouncer at a saloon somewhere in Queens. But he got let go, for obvious reasons."

"Yeah, I'll say. Just what every bar needs: an employee who roughs up the would-be customers. So what is Jameson doing for a living now?"

"My man at the *Daily News* isn't sure, but thinks he's a night watchman at a manufacturing plant or a warehouse in Long Island City."

"Well, at least that may keep him out of the bars at night, but it's a sad downward spiral for someone who used to make headlines, and usually in a positive way."

"Absolutely," Saul said. "For what it's worth, my source says Jameson has never stopped hating your boss. He apparently rips into Wolfe whenever he's got an audience in a bar. Still says he'll get even with him someday."

"Given the guy's track record in life these last few years, that sounds like an empty threat."

"I would agree, Archie, although Jameson does have a group of apparently loyal friends among his drinking buddies. How smart they are is a whole different story."

"Good point. Anything else to report?"

"No, sorry. As I said before, I'm afraid I haven't been able to cross anyone off your 'top five' list."

"At least we know a little more about all of them now. I'll fill Wolfe in and get back to you with any further instructions."

CHAPTER 7

Ten minutes after I hung up with Saul, the phone rang. I had a feeling about the call, and I was right.

"Ah, Mr. Goodwin, at home, I see. And I presume Mr. Wolfe is upstairs with his orchids, as is usual at this time of the morning."

"Do you wish to speak to Mr. Wolfe?" I asked, keeping my voice cool and businesslike.

"No, I felt this was a good chance to speak to you, one man to another. You have not been seen outside your dwelling lately." The statement was followed by a rasping chuckle, or perhaps it was an asthmatic cough.

"I do get out on occasion."

"Really? Such is not what I have been led to understand of late. Also, I am told the unmarked police vehicle that had been parked at one end of your block for several days is no longer there. How do you feel about that?"

"State your business. Strange as it may seem to you, I have work to do."

"Are you this terse and testy with all of the callers to Mr. Wolfe's office?" Another humorless laugh.

"Fortunately, most of our callers do not waste my time."

"I assure you it is not my intent to waste your time—what you have left of it, Mr. Goodwin."

"I repeat, state your business."

"All in good time, Mr. Goodwin, all in good time. I have a habit, some might say a bad habit, of wanting to learn more about an individual I am soon to have, shall we say, a close and final association with."

"You make it sound like you're a hit man."

"A crude phrase, Mr. Goodwin, and not one to my liking."

"Oh, dear. Sorry to upset you, Mr. . . . ?"

"If you are trying to keep me on the line so you can trace this call, don't bother. It won't get you anywhere."

"I have more important business than figuring out where you are at the moment. Good-bye," I told him, cradling the phone and checking my watch. I went out through the kitchen to the rear door and down the passageway, stationing myself in front of the auto repair operation on Thirty-Fourth. I had waited no more than five minutes when a Yellow Cab pulled up to the curb and Cordelia Hutchinson stepped out gingerly.

I could not quarrel with Lily's description of the young lady as "prissy." She wore a navy blue suit over a frilly white blouse and was shod in matching blue pumps. A pillbox hat that covered most of her blond hair and white gloves completed the "straight-from-Miss-Millicent's-Finishing-School" look. Her turned-up nose could be termed cute, but was too short for my taste, and her chin showed signs of receding in later years. Her wide-eyed expression suggested a total lack of guile, although I had had enough experience with women not to be taken in by facial appearances.

"Good morning," I said, flashing a grin. "You are Miss Hutchinson."

"And you must be Mr. Goodwin," she replied with an exaggerated flutter of lashes and a batting of light blue eyes as she held out a gloved hand. If this was flirting, she was not good at it.

"Guilty as charged. Please follow me." I led her along the passageway to our door.

"I never realized private detectives operated this way," she said as we entered the kitchen, "although I appreciate your concern about my privacy."

"This is not unusual. Welcome to our world," I said as I ushered her past Fritz, who ignored us pointedly as he prepared lunch. I led her down the hall to the office and directed her to the red leather chair. "Mr. Wolfe will be in soon," I said, walking out and closing the door behind me.

I was in the hall when I heard the noise of the descending elevator. "Miss Hutchinson is planted in the office awaiting your arrival," I told Wolfe when he stepped out of the car.

He made a face, as he often does at the prospect of having to work. "I had a call this morning from our new friend," I said, "but I will tell you about it later." I returned to the office, followed seconds later by Wolfe, who detoured around the desk and deposited himself in his favorite chair, placing a raceme of orchids in a vase on the blotter and ringing for beer.

If our guest was surprised by Wolfe's dimensions, she did not show it.

"Miss Hutchinson," he said, dipping his chin. "Would you like something to drink? Coffee, perhaps?" he asked as I slipped in behind my desk.

"No, thank you, sir," she replied, gloved hands clasped in her lap and ankles pressed tightly together. "I appreciate your agreeing to see me. It has taken me a long time to get up the courage to call you, or rather, Mr. Goodwin here."

Wolfe considered her as he opened the first of two beers Fritz brought in. "You are being blackmailed." It was not a question.

She nodded. "Yes, sir. I guess you could say that I am now paying for my sins."

"As we all do eventually, in one form or another. Continue."

"You probably know that my family is well known and . . . successful. I have been given every advantage in life." She turned to me. "May I have a glass of water, please?"

I went to the kitchen, and when I returned with the water, Cordelia was in mid-sentence.

". . . and during my time in Italy—Florence, it was—I met a man who, well, who I became friendly with." She actually blushed.

"How long did this friendship last?" Wolfe asked.

"From March until early May of this year, I am sorry to say. This man, he comes from a Florentine family that has been in the fine leather business for centuries. They have an elegant old villa in the hills above the city. He is more than ten years older than I am, and very charming, as so many Italians are, and . . ." She lifted her narrow shoulders and let them fall in a gesture of helplessness.

"Is this man married?"

Cordelia shook her head. "But that is not the real issue, Mr. Wolfe. Before I went to Europe, I reached an understanding with a wonderful boy right here in New York. His name is Lanny Mercer, from the family that builds those expensive airplanes for private companies. You probably have heard of the family."

"What is the extent of this understanding with Mr. Mercer?"

"That we were to announce our engagement in the autumn,

about two months from now. But that was before everything happened." She drank water and dabbed her lips with a lace-trimmed handkerchief. Wolfe waited for her to continue.

"The first letter came a week ago," she went on. "It shocked me so much that I became . . . sort of paralyzed. I told Lanny that I wanted to delay announcing our engagement formally for a while, although I didn't give him a reason."

"How did he react?"

"Oh, he was wonderful about it, Mr. Wolfe, absolutely wonderful, as I would have expected. He told me that if I needed more time, I should take it, marriage being such a big step."

Wolfe drew in air and exhaled. "You mentioned to Mr. Goodwin that you had letters. Do you have them with you?"

She nodded, reached into her purse, and pulled out two sheets, the first of which she handed to Wolfe. He scanned it and set it on the corner of his desk so that I could read it as well. The paper was ordinary white stock, the type sold in drug and stationery stores. The message was neatly printed in black ink, block letters capitalized.

DEAR MISS HUTCHINSON

YOU COME ACROSS TO MOST PEOPLE AS A VERY PROPER YOUNG LADY BUT SOME OF US KNOW BETTER. ONE WONDERS HOW MR LANCE MERCER AND HIS FAMILY WOULD REACT IF THEY KNEW ABOUT YOUR ACTIVITIES WITH A CERTAIN GENTLEMAN IN A CERTAIN HISTORIC ITALIAN CITY? IT IS FULLY IN YOUR POWER TO AVOID THEIR LEARNING OF YOUR ADVENTURE. KEEP WATCHING YOUR MAILBOX.

"I don't know why the foul person who wrote this did not just come right out and ask for money in that letter," Cordelia said, pouting.

"Blackmailers often like to make their victims sweat," I told her. "It's a way to soften them up before making specific demands. When did you hear next?"

"Three days later, but this time there was a phone call. It was a man's muffled voice that I didn't recognize. He told me I would be getting another letter shortly. I tried to ask questions, but he hung up before I could get a word out."

Wolfe finished his first beer, setting the glass down. "The voice was muffled because the caller was disguising it. And the second piece of mail?"

"It arrived yesterday." Cordelia laid another sheet and a photograph on the desk, sliding them toward Wolfe. This time I got up and went around behind him, looking over his shoulder. The block printing was similar to that in the earlier note.

> DEAR MISS HUTCHINSON
>
> THE ENCLOSED PICTURE—WE HAVE OTHERS ALMOST IDENTICAL TO IT—INDICATES HOW SERIOUS WE ARE. WE WILL TURN ALL OF THE PHOTOGRAPHS OVER TO YOU AFTER RECEIVING PAYMENT OF SEVENTY-FIVE THOUSAND DOLLARS IN USED CURRENCY, FIFTY AND ONE-HUNDRED DOLLAR BILLS. WE KNOW YOU HAVE ACCESS TO FUNDS OF THIS SIZE—AND MORE. WE ARE BEING LENIENT WITH YOU. YOU WILL RECEIVE INSTRUCTIONS BY TELEPHONE IN THE NEXT FEW DAYS AS TO WHERE THE MONEY IS TO BE DELIVERED. IF YOU CHOOSE NOT TO COOPERATE, ONE OF THE

PHOTOGRAPHS WILL BE DELIVERED TO THE MERCER FAMILY, ANOTHER TO YOUR PARENTS, AND OTHERS TO THE VARIOUS NEW YORK NEWSPAPERS. AS YOU CAN SEE FROM THE PHOTO, YOU ARE MOST RECOGNIZABLE.

Cordelia certainly was recognizable. The black-and-white print showed her in profile, in the arms of a dark-haired man in what seemed to be a park-like setting. The embrace was not typical of those between casual friends. Her head was thrown back, her mouth open, and her companion was nuzzling her neck, while his hand was in what might be termed an inappropriate place. Although both were fully clothed, it was no stretch to imagine that this dalliance was a prelude to something more intimate.

"It does not appear that this photograph has been doctored," Wolfe said, continuing to study it.

"No, sir, I am afraid it was not," Cordelia said.

"Where was this taken?"

"The Boboli Gardens in Florence. A beautiful place."

"I was there once, many years ago," Wolfe said. "Do you have any idea who the photographer was?"

She shook her head. "None whatever. I did not dream that we were being spied on. We thought we were completely alone in a corner of the gardens."

"Clearly," I said. "Whoever shot the pictures probably was some distance away using a special lens. The image is quite sharp."

"Too sharp," she said ruefully.

"I trust you have the envelopes these missives arrived in," Wolfe said.

She shook her head. "No, I threw them in the wastebasket."

He raised his eyebrows. "Do you, as the letter states, have access to the kind of money being demanded?"

"Yes, sir, I do. I came into a large inheritance, more than five million dollars, when I turned twenty-one, which was just over three years ago."

"Is that fact widely known?"

"It is no secret, at least within our family and their circle of friends, which probably means others know about it as well. As I am sure you are aware, people can be such awful gossips."

"You have not received the second telephone call?" Wolfe asked.

"Not yet. I keep expecting it."

"Have you decided how you will respond?"

"No, sir. That is partly why I am here—for your advice. And I will pay whatever you ask if you can stop these threats."

"Why have you not talked to the police? They are well equipped to deal with situations like the one you are facing, and they are armed with far more resources than I."

"No! I do not want them involved in any way," Cordelia snapped. "This is a private matter, and I want it kept that way."

"I regret to say that may not be possible, Miss Hutchinson. You tell me you came here for my advice, and I am strongly counseling you to discuss the matter with the police."

She crossed her arms and chewed on her lower lip. "So, I cannot hire you, is that what you are saying?"

"No, it is not. What I am doing is laying out your options," Wolfe said.

"My option is to have you stop this blackmailer. Can you tell me what it will cost me?"

"We may discuss fees later. How did you happen to have an extended stay in Florence?"

"I was an English major in college and spent one semester studying in Britain, but I never had the opportunity to get to Italy during that time. I had minored in Renaissance art, and there is no better place to appreciate it than Florence. Spending time there was something I had wanted to do for a long while, and Lanny encouraged me to go. Actually, I had planned to visit several other Italian cities as well, but when I met . . . *him*, I changed my plans and decided to remain in Florence. I canceled trips to Rome, Siena, and Venice."

"During your stay, did you at any time sense you were being watched?"

"No, and I really was not out in public—certainly not in crowds—all that often with . . . with the man in the photograph—although we did drive in his car out into the countryside a few times. But I do not believe anyone was following us—not that I was suspicious."

Wolfe opened his second beer and poured it, frowning as he watched the foam settle. "Did any of your acquaintances from back home visit you in Florence during your time there?"

"A roommate from my college days—her name is Marlene Peters—had decided at the last minute to come to Europe, and she ended up staying in Florence for a week while I was there. We ended up taking day trips to some of the beautiful old Tuscan hill towns. It was so nice to have her there."

"Did she meet your Italian friend?"

"Yes, the three of us had dinner twice—no, it was three times, I think. And on one occasion, he drove us to some of those hill towns I mentioned."

Wolfe turned to me, as he often does when questioning a woman. Years ago, he got it in his mind that I was an expert on what he refers to as the "vagaries of the female sex," and nothing I have said to the contrary can budge him from that belief. It was clear that he wanted me to take over the probing.

"Was your friend Marlene aware of the nature of your relationship with this man?" I asked.

She took a deep breath. "I didn't . . . spell it out to her, of course, but it was obvious that he and I had become close. She never asked me directly, though. He was as attentive to me all during the time the three of us were together as he was when we were alone."

"Does anyone else know about this friendship, any members of your family, for instance?"

"No! None of them—at least not that I'm aware of. It would be terrible if they found out."

"And you had no other acquaintances in Florence?"

"None other than Marlene for those few days and . . . him."

"Enough with pronouns. What is his name?"

Cordelia put her head down. "I would rather not say," she said in a voice just above a whisper.

"Come now, Miss Hutchinson, this is hardly a time to become coy," I said. "You want Mr. Wolfe to find out who is blackmailing you, and presumably to stop this individual. We need to know as much as we can about the principals in this case. You already told us the man you met is part of a wealthy old family in the fine leather business. Why stop there?"

She took a deep breath. "He is Carlo Veronese. You may have heard of the House of Veronese. Their purses are world famous—and very expensive."

"In fact, I do know about them, but only through a woman of my acquaintance who happens to like them," I said. "Tell us more about him."

"He is, well, very good-looking, and as I said before, several years older than me. I now know that I—"

"You must excuse me," Wolfe said, getting to his feet. "I have another appointment, Miss Hutchinson. Mr. Goodwin will continue gathering information from you, and he and I will confer later. You will be hearing from us."

CHAPTER 8

Cordelia watched Wolfe leave the room, then turned to me in dismay. "Did I say something to upset him?"

"By no means. That is very normal behavior for Mr. Wolfe. He is brusque by nature and he has many projects going on at the same time," I improvised. "You don't mind my asking you some more questions, do you?"

"Oh no, not at all, Mr. Goodwin, not at all. I did not mean in any way to suggest that."

"Good. When Mr. Wolfe left, you had mentioned that Carlo Veronese is very good-looking and quite a bit older than you. You started to say 'I now know that I' . . . and then you were interrupted."

She blushed. "Yes, what I was going to say was, I now know I allowed myself to be taken in by his looks and his charm. I could tell you that the beauty of Florence affected my actions, but that would be a feeble excuse. I know myself that well."

"We all get carried away at one time or another, Miss Hutchinson," I said in my most sympathetic tone.

"Please, call me Cordelia."

"Only if you call me Archie. So, what were the circumstances of your meeting this charming man?"

"Please do not make fun of me, Mr.—Archie."

"I assure you, I am not. I make it a point never to make fun of anyone—other than myself, of course."

"You are very nice . . . Archie, like I knew you would be from the way you sounded on the telephone," she said, placing slender, manicured fingers on my arm. "As to how we met: It was my second or third day in Florence. I was strolling on the Ponte Vecchio, which is a famous old bridge over the Arno River that has beautiful shops lining it. I was looking at a purse in the window of a leather-goods store when he—Carlo—came up behind me and leaned over my shoulder. 'Do you like that?' he asked, pointing at the purse.

"I was startled, but I was aware of the reputation Italian men have for being, well, forward. I told him I thought the purse was very lovely and tasteful.

"'I am so very glad you think so, *signorina*. My mother designed it,' he said, bowing. 'Let us go in. You can take a better look at it.' So we went into the little shop, where the saleswoman called him by name and fussed over him."

"Did you buy the purse?"

"No, but Carlo and I ended up talking, and I found that I, well . . . I enjoyed his company. He insisted on treating me to a drink at a beautiful little café along the Arno."

"Did he have to insist forcefully?"

"Well, no, I can't lie, least of all to myself."

"I have to ask you this question, Cordelia. Didn't you at some point during your relationship suspect that Mr. Veronese just might have used the same approach before with other window-shopping young women, particularly ones who were visitors to the city like yourself?"

"I really wasn't thinking at the time," she said, shaking her head. "I just wasn't. I can't really claim it was the romantic surroundings that affected me. I don't know what else to tell you. Maybe I am just weak-willed, Archie."

I passed on that comment. "Just how did your relationship with Mr. Veronese come to an end?"

"After we had been seeing each other for several weeks—as I said before, I had extended my stay in Florence because of him—he told me that we should not see each other anymore. It came as a total surprise to me."

"Did he give a reason?"

I thought she was going to break into tears, but she controlled herself, hands clenched. "He said it was not realistic for us to think anything could come of our *grande amore*—that's what he called it, *un grande amore*, I think I have that right. But at that moment, I finally realized it was something very different, Archie, something hardly grand, if you understand me. It was as if I had been slapped into coming to my senses."

"All right, let's move on. I am assuming you do not want to pay the blackmailer, or else you would not have come to Mr. Wolfe. But you also don't want word of your dalliance to be made public, certainly not to the Mercers. Now, I am the first to recognize Mr. Wolfe's genius, but even given his talents, you may not be able to accomplish both of these ends. Perhaps one or the other. And even if you do ante up, who is to say the blackmailer won't come back for more? There may be dozens of copies of that photograph, or other photos nearly identical to it, as that one note suggested."

"It's really that bad, isn't it, Archie?" Cordelia shivered, although the room was warm.

"It is not good. Do you have any candidates for the blackmailer, anyone who has a particular reason to dislike you or perhaps be jealous of you? Or someone in need of a large sum?"

"I really cannot think of a soul who would stoop to such nasty tactics. I've never hurt anyone in my life, at least not that I am aware of."

"I believe you, Cordelia. However, you are wealthy, and someone wants to get a chunk of that wealth."

"But who in Florence could it have been? Not my old roommate—we are very close. I consider her my best friend. And certainly not Carlo, who comes from money himself, probably as much as or more than I have."

"Let us not limit ourselves to people in Florence. Someone from here could have learned what was going on between you and Veronese and hired an individual over there to shadow you and take pictures. From what I have read, there are plenty of Italian photographers who specialize in just this sort of work and are very good at it. I'm sure you've heard the word *paparazzi*."

"Yes, those horrible men who chase after movie stars and other famous people." She clenched her fists again.

"And they are not just limited to Italy. We've got our share of those sleazy picture-takers right here in New York, too," I said, then added, "I've been meaning to ask about your family. Do you have brothers and sisters?"

"Two of each, all of them several years older than me. I'm told I was something of a surprise," she said.

"A nice surprise for your parents, I'm sure."

She smiled for the first time since she had arrived. "I have always been very close to both of them."

"I'm glad to hear it. And also with your siblings?"

"We're not really all that close, I suppose because of the age differences. I don't see most of them all that often, except Tom."

"Where do they live and what do they do?"

"Annie, she's the oldest, is an advertising copywriter, single, and lives over in Brooklyn. She's had several boyfriends, but broke up with each of them. She's very fussy—too fussy, if you ask me. Tom, the next oldest, is also single now, and he's currently staying with us on Sutton Place, which is why I see more of him than the others. He got divorced a few months ago, and their split was not pleasant. The settlement with his ex-wife became somewhat nasty.

"My other sister, Kathleen Willis, is recently divorced from her husband, a bond trader, and she lives in Westport, Connecticut, in a beautiful house. She has two children. And then there's Doug, the youngest except for me. He's one of those starving artists you hear about. He's never been married, although he's had several relationships. I even introduced him to Marlene, my old roommate, and they went out a couple of times, but that didn't seem to work out—though neither of them ever talked to me about it."

"Where does Doug live?"

"He has a somewhat shabby loft in Greenwich Village—or so I understand, I've never seen it—and he struggles to sell his paintings. I've seen just a few of them, and I shouldn't be saying this about my brother, but I really don't think he's terribly talented."

"You referred to him as a 'starving artist.' He can't be too hard up if he got an inheritance like you did."

"Doug has burned through a lot of it, almost all of it, I'm afraid. He invested in an import-export company that one of his college classmates started, and it was a colossal failure. Neither Doug nor his friend has much business sense. My father urged him not to get involved in the venture, but, well, you know how offspring are about taking their parents' advice."

"I do. I had my share of arguments with my father, although now I can see he was right more often than I was."

"Well, Dad and Doug are still not on the best of terms over the whole sad business. What about my fee, Archie? I brought my checkbook." She pulled it out of her purse and started to open it.

"As Mr. Wolfe said before, that can wait. And as I told you, he does not come cheap. How did you hear about him?"

"I've seen his name—and yours, too—in the newspapers several times. From what I have read, he seems to have a very good record at . . . at solving things."

"He does. I assume no one knows you have approached him."

"No, just my diary knows. I was alone in my bedroom at my parents' home on Sutton Place both of the times I telephoned you. What's next, Archie?"

"At some point, we probably will have to talk both to your parents and to your brothers and sisters."

She jerked upright. "You can't do that, Archie! You must not. They—especially my mother and father—would be crushed. They must never know about what has happened."

"Surely your parents love you very much. Wouldn't they understand?"

"I . . . maybe. But I couldn't bear telling them, particularly my father," she said, as if she were beginning to hyperventilate. "I've always been, well, his favorite, probably because I came along later. And as for my brothers and sisters, I just don't want them to know either."

"It's possible that the blackmailers already have approached one or more members of your family," I told her. "We need to know if that is the case."

Cordelia shook her head vigorously. "No, Archie, no!"

"All right, let me ask this. Do you have something—say, an expensive piece of jewelry—that you are particularly fond of?"

She threw me a puzzled look. "Well, yes I do. Why?"

"What is it?"

"A diamond necklace. My father gave it to me when I had my coming-out party around my eighteenth birthday. I treasure it more than anything else I own."

"Did the necklace go along with you to Italy?"

"Oh no, I was afraid something might happen to it."

"Did your parents or siblings know whether you took it on the trip?"

She wrinkled her forehead. "I don't think the subject ever came up. Why do you ask?"

"Because perhaps we can develop a scenario in which you did have the necklace in Florence. And it got stolen from your hotel room."

"I don't understand."

"We could make the stolen necklace the reason you're being blackmailed."

Cordelia shook her head. "Please pardon me for saying so, Archie, but that seems awfully far-fetched."

I shrugged. "Maybe, but let me bounce it off Mr. Wolfe. I'll talk to him about the necklace idea, and whether he likes it or not, he will decide how you should respond when you receive instructions from the blackmailer, which could be any time—possibly today or tomorrow."

"But I am still not officially a client, am I?"

"No, although I'll do what I can to plead your case."

"Thank you, Archie. Should I telephone later?" she asked.

"Why don't I call you, or is that a problem? Will someone else answer?"

"Probably the maid, Sheila. If she asks who is on the line, and she probably will, you can tell her you are from the DeVane Jewelers. They're resetting a ring for me, so a call from them would be expected."

"I'm sure I can sound like a jeweler. Now, how are you going to get home? I can call a taxi and have it pick you up over on Thirty-Fourth Street."

"No, that is not necessary," she said, standing and smoothing a skirt that didn't need smoothing. "I love to walk, and it gives me a chance to think. Heaven knows, I have a lot of thinking to do."

We exited through the kitchen, Fritz ignoring us once more, and I escorted Cordelia down the passageway. When we got to the street, we shook hands and I told her she would be hearing from me. I watched as she walked away and wondered where her thoughts were taking her.

CHAPTER 9

When I returned to the office, Wolfe was seated behind his desk again. "Well, that was one cute trick," I told him as I dropped into my own chair. "Running off and hiding in the kitchen while I questioned the young lady. What were you out doing there, harassing poor Fritz again about whether or not chives should be used in tomato tarts?"

"I never harass Fritz."

"Hah! Of course you do, let me count the ways. For starters, there was the episode with the onions in the shad roe, and—"

"Twaddle!"

"No, sir, not twaddle. Anyway, you certainly shifted into what for you represents high gear on your way out the door. Afraid the ever-so-demure Miss Hutchinson was going to make a pass at you?"

"Are you quite through, Mr. Goodwin?"

"Yeah, I am, at least on the subject of your hightailing it out of the office as though you were running away from a horde of rampaging elephants. But I also noticed that you did your best to talk her out of hiring us. A man would think you didn't need the money."

"I merely explained the situation to her. I believe you will agree that she is owed that much from us."

"Okay, if that's your story, you should by all means stick to it. What do you think of our potential client?"

He made a face. "A naïf, an emotional child."

"Agreed, but an extremely rich one. Do we proceed?"

"How much of what she told us do you think is veracious?" As I mentioned earlier, Wolfe somehow got it in his head years ago that I am an expert on women, and that that expertise extends to my ability to detect anything untrue or misleading that is spoken by a member of the female species.

"Maybe eighty percent, or slightly less," I said. "For one, I have to wonder whether her breakup with the Italian Don Juan happened as she described it. I also have to question the depth of her commitment to young Mr. Mercer, he of the airplane manufacturing millions. It seems to me that she was very easily wooed by the Italian gentleman—if he can be so termed. Actually, *gigolo* comes to mind as an apt description."

"Hardly the correct usage of the word," Wolfe chided. "In most definitions, a gigolo is one who lives off the wealth of a woman. In this instance, it would appear that Mr. Veronese is in possession of substantial wealth of his own."

I sighed. "Okay, would you accept *cad*? Or maybe *rogue*?"

Wolfe shrugged. "Just before Miss Hutchinson arrived, you mentioned a telephone call from that man. Also, have you heard from Saul?"

I gave Wolfe a verbatim report on my brief conversation with our nameless pest, then filled him in on Saul's findings and my conversation with Cordelia after he had left the room. He was silent for more than a minute, then came forward in his chair. "Confound it, let Miss Hutchinson know we will attempt to locate and stop her blackmailer. But make it clear to her that we cannot proceed without speaking to members of her family and possibly to other acquaintances of hers as well. Be firm about this."

"I am always firm. But you know the young lady will not like that."

"Of course she won't. She seems determined to keep her Italian indiscretion from those closest to her. But the young woman said at least one sensible thing when she sat in that chair."

"That we pay for our sins?"

"Precisely, and part of her payment must almost surely be the exposure of her liaison, at least if she has any hope of avoiding blackmail."

"She may not go along with it."

"Then my hands are tied," Wolfe said, turning both palms up. "As you know very well, I will not undertake any investigation that restricts our ability to question those who may have pertinent information."

"What if we concoct a scenario in which Cordelia takes a valuable diamond necklace—a treasured gift from her father—on the trip to Italy, and it gets lifted from her hotel room? We can use that in our questioning of the family as the reason for the blackmail. And we could—"

"Utter nonsense!" Wolfe spat. "You know better than to propose such a preposterous contrivance. Is it necessary for me to point out its fallacies to you?"

"Okay, so maybe I was reaching a bit," I said. "Cordelia didn't think the idea was so hot, either."

"That much speaks well for her. She is—yes, what is it, Fritz?"

"Pardon me for interrupting," he said from the doorway, "but this morning, I was dusting in the front room, and I found something you should see."

"Can't you bring whatever it is in here?"

"No, sir, I cannot."

Wolfe frowned and pursed his lips. "Very well," he grumped, reluctantly levering himself upright. "Show us."

We walked into the front room, and a stern-faced Fritz pointed at the window, which looks out onto Thirty-Fifth Street. About halfway up the pane, there were two circular indentations, although the glass had not been broken. Wolfe looked questioningly at me.

"Yeah, made by bullets, and judging by the size, from a thirty-two. I can probably find the shells under the window."

"No, do not go outside, Archie," said Wolfe. "For the moment, we will stipulate that we have been fired upon. Did you hear anything last night, Fritz?"

"No, sir."

"Probably a silencer. It's a good thing we had bulletproof glass installed some years back," I said.

"Not bulletproof, bullet-*resistant*," Wolfe corrected. "As you are well aware, no glass can be made completely impenetrable. Had someone wanted to puncture that window, he could easily have found a firearm strong enough to accomplish the job."

"So this is another warning?"

"Clearly. The front room is almost never occupied, so the shots that were fired, even had they entered the room, likely would not have been lethal."

"But for the sake of argument, how would our anonymous shooter know the front room doesn't get used much?" I asked.

"Unfortunately, a feature several years ago in the *Times* went into great detail about our operations, including the layout of the house," Wolfe said. "As you may remember, none of us—including you and Fritz—agreed to talk to the writer. But unnamed sources, probably clients or suspects who had been here, provided a great deal of detail, especially about the first floor."

"Oh, yeah, I'd forgotten about that damned piece, or else I put it out of my mind," I said.

Fritz looked nervously from Wolfe to me and back again during our conversation, like someone watching a tennis match. "Does this mean we will have to leave here?" he asked.

"Not at the moment," Wolfe replied, "although it is possible that at some point we will temporarily relocate. For now, however, we shall stand our ground and take the necessary precautions."

Wolfe's statement was meant to be reassuring, but one look at Fritz Brenner's face was enough to realize those words had not achieved the desired effect. When we were seated back in the office and Fritz had returned to the kitchen, Wolfe turned to me. "Fritz is understandably shaken. Do you feel the same way?"

"Well, it is hardly a picnic to realize someone is targeting you. But am I about to jump ship? Of course not. I say we stick it out right here and learn who's got it in for us, or rather, for me."

"Would you suggest we abandon any thoughts of trying to identify Miss Hutchinson's blackmailer and concentrate on the individual who seeks to bedevil us? Note that I use the plural pronoun."

"Call me an old softy, but I've grown fond of our young Cordelia—oh, not in a romantic sense, mind you. She's hardly my type, but she is something of a damsel in distress. And at the risk of sounding crass, she is rich and, like it or not, we need money."

Wolfe leaned back and closed his eyes. They were still closed three minutes later when the doorbell rang.

I went down the hall, saw the figure through the glass in the front door, and returned to the office. “Cramer,” I said.

Wolfe opened his eyes and raised his brows. “Again? All right, let him in.”

I followed orders, and after he marched down the hall to the office, the inspector planted his substantial fundament in the red leather chair and glowered at Wolfe. “Well?” he barked.

“‘Well’ indeed, Mr. Cramer. I had not expected to see you so soon after your last visit.”

“I hadn’t expected to be here again myself, but you have a way of attracting attention.”

“I assure you such is not my intent.”

“Uh-huh. Whether you know it or not—and I suspect you do—shots were fired at one of your windows sometime within the last day, probably last night.”

“Extraordinary,” Wolfe said.

“Isn’t it? Ever since the other shots were fired at Goodwin that night, we have had this house under surveillance. And this morning about six, the men in one of our cars passing by spotted two circular impressions, caused by bullets, in the window of your front room.”

“How do you know they were caused by bullets?” Wolfe asked.

“These were found under the window,” Cramer said, reaching into his suit jacket pocket and pulling out two shell casings, which he laid on the desk blotter. “They’re thirty-two caliber and could’ve been fired from either a revolver or an automatic. Interesting that those earlier shells were also thirty-twos. Or would you term that ‘extraordinary,’ too?”

“I suppose I should be flattered at your concern for our welfare,” Wolfe said. “Would you like something to drink?”

“No, thanks, and please don’t flatter yourself. The department’s concern is for the safety of everyone who passes by and lives on this block, not just you and Goodwin. Care to tell me now what this is all about?"

"Over the years, I have made numerous enemies, which is hardly a surprise to you. Apparently, one or more of them now seeks retribution."

"You seem very calm about the whole business," Cramer snorted. "Do you have any clue as to who that might be?"

"No, I do not."

"To repeat a question I asked on my last visit: Are you now working on a case?" I smiled inwardly at how my boss would answer.

"At the moment, I do not have a commission," Wolfe stated.

"So you say. And you have no idea who's after your scalp, not even an educated guess?"

Wolfe sighed and placed his hands, palms down, on the desk. "Mr. Goodwin and I are now in the process of reviewing past cases in an attempt to determine who might most wish us ill."

"That could be one long list," Cramer deadpanned. "Let us know if you want help from the department."

"That is a most generous offer, sir."

"Not really. If anything happens to you, all hell will break loose in the press, and from the commissioner on down, we will be roundly castigated for failing to protect New York's best-known private investigator. For instance, I can only imagine how the *Gazette*, your buddy Lon Cohen's paper, would react. They would probably call for my head, but what else is new? They and the other papers have been doing that off and on for years."

"Thank you for putting the situation in perspective," Wolfe said.

"My pleasure," the inspector responded, with no pleasure whatsoever evident in his tone. He rose slowly and walked out of the office and down the hall, and I followed along, bolting the door behind him.

CHAPTER 10

So, you claim we have no commission at the moment," I said to Wolfe after Cramer had departed. "That news will come as something of a surprise to our Miss Hutchinson."

"I did not lie to the inspector; we have yet to accept any payment from the young woman."

"All right, split hairs if it pleases you. By the way, you said early on that we must remain vigilant. But shots were fired at our window—presumably, although not necessarily, in the night—and the police retrieved the shell casings from under said window without our knowledge that any of this was happening."

Wolfe looked up from his book. "Would you prefer that I bring Saul and Fred in so the three of you can keep watch in eight-hour shifts around the clock?"

"Well, at least that is one plan of action, sort of. What else do we have at the moment?"

"Confound it, must I always—" Wolfe was interrupted by the telephone, which I answered.

"Archie, the call just came—the blackmailer!" It was a breathless Cordelia Hutchinson. "And he, and he . . ."

"Okay, slow down and tell me exactly what the man said," I told her, signaling to Wolfe to pick up his instrument.

"He told me . . . what I have to do. He was most insistent and most specific. I'm still shaking from the conversation."

"Go on."

"He wants the money, in fifty-and one-hundred dollar bills, delivered to a spot in Central Park."

"When?" I asked.

"He said tonight, but I told him I wasn't sure I could get seventy-five thousand dollars that soon. He said he would call me again later today with more specifics. And he said that if I couldn't get the money at all, the pictures would be sent to my family and the Mercers, and to the newspapers."

"Do you believe you can get the money?"

"I . . . think so. I have a personal banker at our family's bank, Amalgamated Trust, and he has always been extremely cooperative in the past."

"Given the size of your account and those of others in your family, I am hardly surprised. But won't this request throw him, particularly when you ask for used currency?"

"If he asks, which I doubt, I will tell him that I plan to purchase an expensive automobile, and that I don't want to have to bother with a car loan that has monthly payments. I will also tell him that the car dealer prefers to receive the payment in this manner."

"Interesting. With that kind of dough, you could be getting yourself a Rolls-Royce," I said.

"That would not be so surprising, Archie. After all, my father has driven them for years."

"Like father, like daughter. Okay, when will you know if you will be able to get the dough?"

"I have an appointment with Mr. Harkness—he's the banker at Amalgamated—this afternoon. But Archie, I still haven't paid you anything." I looked at Wolfe, who shook his head.

"Never mind that for now. We can discuss the payment later. Just call us and let us know when you can get the money."

"I will, Archie, and . . . thank you."

"Well, do we have anything resembling a plan?" I asked Wolfe after we had cradled our instruments.

He leaned back and studied the ceiling. "We will apprehend the blackmailer," he said.

"By 'we' you mean me, of course."

"Along with Saul and Fred, assuming they agree."

Earlier, I referred to Fred Durkin as one member of our poker group. As a private investigator, he isn't in the same league with Saul Panzer, but then nobody is. Fred's far from brilliant, but he is both brave and loyal, and he would jump off a cliff if Wolfe asked him to. Oh, and I should mention that he saved my life once during a stakeout that became a shootout in a darkened warehouse one night across the East River from Manhattan. Enough said.

"Do you want me to get the boys now?"

"No, we shall wait until we have heard from Miss Hutchinson. It is time for lunch."

After a meal of sweetbreads in béchamel sauce with beet and watercress salad, followed by spiced brandied cherries, we were back in the office having coffee when the phone rang. We both picked up our receivers as I recited my usual, "Nero Wolfe's office, Archie Goodwin speaking."

"I will have the money tomorrow morning," Cordelia said, sounding like she was out of breath.

"Have you been running?"

"No, I am just nervous, Archie. Very nervous."

"Miss Hutchinson, can you recite to us precisely what instructions were given to you by the presumed blackmailer?" It was Wolfe talking.

"He told me to bring the money in a case to Central Park. He said that when he calls back, he will tell me the exact location."

"Did he stipulate that you had to be the one bringing the money, or can you appoint an agent to execute it?"

"I don't know, Mr. Wolfe. Do you want me to ask him?"

"Yes, and try to insist that someone else deliver the money."

"What if he asks who that person is?"

"Just tell him that it is a very good friend, someone you place a great deal of trust in. Tell him you are simply too frightened to carry out the delivery yourself, that you are afraid you would make a hash of it."

"That would be the truth," she said.

"Please telephone us immediately upon hearing from the man," Wolfe told her.

"I am, of course, that 'very good friend' of hers," I said after we had hung up.

"Unless you would rather let the cup pass from you."

"No, I am already the target of one person. What's one more? In for a penny, in for a pound."

"I am most impressed that you are conversant with that ancient English adage," Wolfe said.

"Don't be, I learned it from you. Besides, this little project of ours may just take my mind off whomever it is who wants to see me sent back to my relatives in Ohio in a pine box."

Wolfe chose not to reply, ringing for beer and opening his latest book. I turned to my desk and began typing letters he had dictated that morning.

Cordelia's call came at four-fifteen, which of course meant Wolfe was up in the plant rooms on the roof with Theodore Horstmann, communing with his orchids in his second session of the day.

"I have my instructions," she said, her voice still shaky.

"Fire away, I'm taking notes." This was one time I did not want to entrust the details to my memory.

"He wants the money delivered tomorrow night, at ten o'clock. 'Precisely at ten,' he insisted. He was very definite about that. In the park, about a hundred fifty yards east of the corner of Central Park West and Seventy-Seventh Street, there is a blue spruce, the tallest tree in a cluster, he told me. He said the money, in an attaché case or suitcase—he doesn't care what type it is—should be placed at the base of that tree on its east side."

"Did he say you had to be the one to put it there?"

"Oh—no, he said that it could be someone I trusted, he didn't seem to care who. But he told me that if the money was not brought to that spot, and at the time he specified, the pictures would be sent immediately."

"Did he—or you—say anything else?"

"Just that once he had received the money, a package of photographs would be sent to me, special delivery."

"In an envelope either with no return address or a phony address, of course. Okay, Cordelia. I will talk to Mr. Wolfe and get back to you. I will call on that number you gave me."

"Do you have any idea when that will be?"

"Just stay near the phone," I told her. "We still have almost thirty hours before the delivery."

After signing off with Cordelia, I climbed the three flights of stairs to the plant rooms on the roof. As often as I have stepped into these rooms over the years, I never get over the awesome experience of seeing ten thousand orchids in every color of the rainbow—and maybe some hues that have never even made it onto a rainbow.

Several years ago, the *Gazette* proposed running a special Sunday magazine section filled with color photos of the orchids, but Wolfe turned them down flat, and even Lon Cohen's intercession on behalf of his employer couldn't budge him.

Upon finishing the climb, one first encounters the cool room, with some twenty-five hundred plants, among them *Odontoglossums* on both sides of the aisle in yellow, rose, and white with spots. Next is the intermediate or moderate room, where the splashy *Cattleyas*, in purple, orange, lavender, and yellow, show off shamelessly. Then comes the tropical room, which is filled with *Miltonia* hybrids and *Phalaenopsis* in pinks, greens, and browns.

At the far end of the conservatory, one finds the pottery room, where on this day, Wolfe, in rolled-up shirtsleeves, was with Theodore Horstmann. They were studying a plant in a pot on the bench as intently as two highly trained surgeons about to conduct a delicate operation. As is usually the case when I dare to enter the hallowed plant rooms, Horstmann glared at me. We have never warmed to each other, and after all these years, it is clear that we never will.

"Yes?" Wolfe snapped at me. He hates to be interrupted during his orchid time, but I felt the day's events warranted the intrusion. I gave him Cordelia's report as he scowled. "Any instructions?" I asked after I had finished.

"Call Saul and Fred. Have them here at nine tonight."

"What if either of them can't make it?"

"Without going into any detail about the meeting, tell them they would be honoring me with their presence."

I began to reply, but he turned back to the plant that was being nursed. I had been dismissed.

CHAPTER 11

I started with Saul, who picked up on the first ring. "Mr. Wolfe said he would be honored by your presence here this evening at nine."

"Getting pretty formal, aren't we? Your boss knows all he has to do is ask, and I'll show up, day or night," he said. "Should I come via the back way again?"

I said yes and called Fred. "Of course I'll be there, Archie," he said. "Anything I need to know ahead of time?"

"No, you'll get filled in when you're here. You know how to get to the brownstone from Thirty-Fourth Street?" I asked.

"Uh, yeah, I do. Don't you remember, one time years back when we were working on the—"

"Yes I do, no time to talk now. See you later."

They arrived simultaneously at eight fifty, and if Fred was puzzled by the back path approach, he didn't indicate it. These two are among the few people with whom Wolfe will shake hands, and following that formality, Saul parked himself in the red leather chair as befits his status with Wolfe, while Fred, who is my height but thicker in the midsection and thinner on his dome, took one of the yellow chairs. I passed out drinks—scotch for Saul and beer for Fred, who thinks that is what he should drink when in Wolfe's presence. I poured myself a scotch.

"Thank you both for coming on such short notice," Wolfe said, looking from one to the other. "I would like to enlist your assistance in an operation, but after hearing my description of its particulars, one or both of you may choose to decline to participate. If so, I fully understand. The situation is not without risks."

"Let's hear it," Saul said, holding up his glass.

"Yeah, I agree," Fred added. "You've always been square with me, Mr. Wolfe, and I want to hear the deal, too."

"Very well," Wolfe said. He proceeded to take them through the Cordelia Hutchinson case from the start.

"Okay, the drop is to take place in the park near Seventy-Seventh and Central Park West, which puts it a stone's throw, or maybe two, east of the Natural History Museum and a little west of that small lake," Saul said. "At ten, that section of the park figures to be pretty deserted, wouldn't you say, Archie?"

"I'd say. But then, we would hardly expect our mystery man to choose the spot because of the crowds."

"Manifestly," Wolfe said. "However, he surely will be on alert as he enters the park in his quest for the money. Archie will have placed the case next to the specified tree and will bide his time nearby. I want our man captured and unharmed. Do all of you feel this is feasible?"

"Chances are he'll be armed," Fred put in.

"And he may very well have a lookout," Saul added.

"Possibly," I said, "but I doubt that he'll be expecting three of us. After all, he presumably does not know that Miss Hutchinson has hired us. We should have the element of surprise in our favor."

Saul nodded. "I think we should triangulate the area, making sure that if there happens to be gunplay, we won't be firing at one another. I also think we should go over and have a look at that spot in the park during the day tomorrow and give it the once-over."

"The blackmailer might be there all day, though, keeping watch," Fred said, his broad brow knitted.

Saul shook his head. "I doubt that, but you may be right. What do you think, Archie?"

"I am not sure our pickup man, whoever he is, will hang around the park all day," I said. "But I do like the idea of us getting an advance look at the scene without tramping all over the place. We could drive up there in the morning and do our reconnaissance from the car, parking it on Central Park West."

"How does that sound?" Wolfe asked, looking at each of us in turn.

Fred nodded after a sip of beer, and Saul grinned, giving a thumbs-up.

"Very well," Wolfe said. "Once again, I stress that this sortie may have its perils. I realize the three of you are hardly strangers to risk, but I do not want unnecessary chances taken." We agreed to be cautious and use discretion.

The next morning at nine, after finishing breakfast under Fritz's watchful eye and somber expression, I left the brownstone by the back door and walked to Curran Motors over on Tenth Avenue, where our cars have been garaged for years. When I got there, I found Saul and Fred waiting on the sidewalk out front.

"You are exactly two minutes and forty-three seconds late," Saul said, making a production out of consulting his wristwatch.

"I was not about to wolf down Fritz's wonderful poached eggs Burgundian," I replied haughtily. "A dish like that must be savored, and the poor man is upset enough lately without my treating his culinary efforts as if they were some slapped-together hash-house grub."

"Point taken," Saul allowed. "You did the humane thing, all right. Now let's hit the road."

Ten minutes later, I was steering the Heron sedan north with Saul riding shotgun and Fred in the rear. We drove up Eighth Avenue to Columbus Circle, where the street's name changes to Central Park West. Another eighteen blocks put us at Seventy-Seventh. I eased the car to the curb on the east side of the street.

"Okay, over there is where we're supposed to leave the money," I said, gesturing to a spot about a hundred yards east of us. "That's the blue spruce. It looks to be just about halfway between Central Park West and that interior road that winds its way through the park."

Saul scratched his chin. "So the question is, from which direction will our man come?"

"I'd guess from the east," Durkin said. "The money is supposed to be put at the base of the tree on its east side, right? And that's the side closest to the park road."

"You may be right, Fred," I said, "but we've got to be prepared for him—I'm assuming it's a him—coming from either direction. I'll put the satchel, or whatever kind of bag our Miss Hutchinson puts the money in, at the base of the tree at nine fifty-eight tonight. Then I'll walk away slowly, heading east toward the park road."

"Which means you may run head-on into the guy as he approaches the spruce," Saul said.

"Maybe so, although I'm guessing that he'll be in hiding, probably behind another tree, until I move away from the satchel. Of course, both of you will be out of sight as well—one to the northeast, the other to the southeast, well away from the tree."

"I'll take the northeast," Saul said. "We will be armed, of course."

I nodded. "You will. But remember Mr. Wolfe's instructions. He is to be taken alive."

"That may not be so easy," Fred said. "Chances are ten-to-one he'll be carrying a piece as well."

"That poses a challenge, all right," I conceded. "But if we can get the drop on him before calling to him, he may not be able to level his weapon. After all, he'll be concentrating on hauling the money away. That kind of a payday has a way of blurring a man's mind."

After our brief reconnaissance, I garaged the Heron and the three of us went to the brownstone, once more via the rear entrance. An agitated Fritz let us in.

"Archie, a lady telephoned twice for you. She did not leave her name but said she would call again. She sounded most excited, and she was most unhappy that you were not here. I told her I did not know when you would return."

"That would be Miss Hutchinson. She'll call again, probably in the next ten minutes or less," I told him. "We will be in the office."

Wolfe was in the midst of his morning communion with the orchids up in the plant rooms as we settled in, me behind my desk, Saul in the red leather chair, and Fred occupying one of the yellow ones. We all were sipping Fritz's excellent coffee when the phone rang.

"Oh, Archie, I am so glad to hear your voice," Cordelia said in her usual breathless tone. "I have it. . . . I have the money, right here, right in front of me. What do we do now? I am so frightened."

I tried without success to calm her down. "What do you have the currency in?" I asked.

"A black leather attaché case."

"We can come and get it from you."

"No, I would rather come to you, Archie."

"Aren't you afraid of venturing out with all that dough?"

"No, I am not. I will have our doorman get me a cab and come straight to that spot on Thirty-Fourth Street where you met me before, if that is all right with you and Mr. Wolfe."

"Okay, but the sooner the better," I told her. She said she would leave Sutton Place in five minutes.

I filled Saul and Fred in. "We should be there when her cab pulls up," I said to them.

"She probably can't wait to be rid of that bundle," Saul said.

We had been on the sidewalk for no more than ten minutes when a Yellow Cab pulled up and Cordelia stepped out with the attaché case. "Have the cab wait," I said after introducing Saul and Fred to her as my trusted associates.

"But I thought I would be coming in with you, Archie."

"Not necessary," I said, taking the case from her. "We will be handling things for you from here on today. Go home and wait to hear from me."

"How will you deal with . . . with tonight?" She chewed on her lower lip and kneaded her hands. At that moment, she had all the poise of a twelve-year-old girl at her first grade-school dance.

"All three of us will be there. You do not have to worry about it."

"Who is going to give him the money, Archie?"

"I am. Leave the details to us, please."

"I just don't want anyone to get hurt."

"No one is going to get hurt. Now go home."

Cordelia did not like the brush-off, but I insisted, telling her again that we had everything planned and in place for tonight.

I practically had to push her back into the taxi, and as it pulled away from the curb, she looked out at me from the rear window, almost in tears.

"The young lady is a nervous wreck," Saul observed. "Can't say that I blame her; she probably wonders what's going to happen to those seventy-five G's she just parted with."

"I think she's plenty more worried about her secret getting out than any possibility of losing the money," I said. "That amount she just coughed up isn't much more than petty cash to her."

Back in the office, we opened the leather case on my desk and took out the bundles of fifties and hundreds. "Somehow it seems like seventy-five grand should take up more space than this," Fred said, handling a few of the stacks of greenbacks.

"Yeah, but it all seems to be here, at least based on a quick eye balling," Saul put in. "I've got to wonder what her bank thought about this."

"Given the size of her family's estate, the bank probably does whatever it gets asked to do by any one of the Hutchinson clan," I said.

"No doubt a prudent response on the part of the financial institution," Nero Wolfe said as he entered the office, fresh from his time up on the roof with the orchids. He nodded to Saul and Fred, then eyed the open attaché case and its contents.

"Looks to be all here," I told him. "Want to count it to make sure?"

He sniffed, sat, and rang for beer. "May I offer anyone a drink?"

We all shook our heads, and I filled Wolfe in on our morning venture to Central Park, as well as our strategy for tonight. "Any thoughts?"

He took a deep breath. "I will answer a question with a question: Do any of you have doubts about the success of this operation?"

"I think we've figured the angles," Saul said. "What we don't know, of course, is how the pickup man will react when he gets called out. And whether he has an accomplice."

"I suppose he could start shooting," Fred put in. "Seventy-five big ones is worth fighting for."

"Indeed it is," Wolfe said. "Archie, your thoughts?"

"The man probably will be situated where he can see me set the case down next to that spruce tree and begin walking away. I won't have a gun showing, and I can't believe he'd risk doing anything that would endanger his getting away with the money."

"Of course, he very well may not be the blackmailer himself, just the courier," Saul pointed out.

I nodded. "True, but whoever he is, he figures to come out of the deal with a nice piece of change."

"Let me briefly review," Wolfe said. "Archie sets the case of money down at the tree and begins to move away to the east, his gait deliberate but slow. The man is sure to emerge quickly from hiding to retrieve his treasure. At that point, Saul and Fred, guns drawn, will converge upon the scene from opposite directions and, if all goes well, they will seize both man and money, and with a modicum of force. Archie will also have reversed his direction, and the three of you will deliver this individual to me. Does anyone have something to add?"

"I think that pretty well covers it," I said, turning to Saul and Fred, both of whom nodded.

"Very well," Wolfe pronounced. "I trust you all will use your intelligence guided by your experience."

This was a line he had used on me many times. We were soon to learn how effective his advice would be.

CHAPTER 12

The predicted heavy rain failed to materialize, with only light showers falling throughout the day. As invariably happens when we are preparing for a critical moment, I found myself on edge, searching for anything that would keep me occupied. I polished three pairs of shoes—two of which did not need it—straightened the neckties in my closet, and dusted the top of my dust-free dresser. In the office, I went back over orchid germination records I had entered onto file cards the day before, thinking I might have made a rare mistake—I hadn't. I looked at my watch several times each hour, always surprised at how slow its hands were moving. And for most of the day, I totally forgot that somewhere out in the vast reaches of the city there dwelled a man with the stated intent to kill me.

Wolfe, as usual in these situations, appeared totally unconcerned about the evening's impending drama. At lunch, he held forth on why third parties have been unsuccessful in most American elections, particularly for president, and at dinner, he took the position that television was singularly responsible for lowering the median IQ of the American populace by between ten and twenty points. I mostly nodded and chewed, not fully appreciating the quality of Fritz's three-star offerings.

Of course, it was somewhat easier for Wolfe to remain calm, given that while Saul, Fred, and I were tramping around in the semi-darkness of the Central Park wilderness, he would be back in the office with a beer and his latest book, or the *New York Times* Sunday crossword puzzle, which he invariably finished.

The hours dragged on after dinner. Finally, at nine, I rose from my desk, stretched, took a drink of water from the glass on my desk, and went to the safe for the shoulder holster and the Marley .32. Wolfe looked up from his book as I strapped the holster and gun under my windbreaker. "I sincerely hope that will not be needed," he said.

"So do I, but tonight I would feel undressed without it. I'm off." I went out the back way with the attaché case full of dough and yet again retrieved the Heron from the garage, driving it to Saul's place on Thirty-Eighth, where he and Fred were waiting in front. We headed north in the drizzle and in silence, the tension palpable.

I parked three blocks south of our destination and we split up. Pedestrian traffic was almost non-existent along Central Park West as I walked north on the east side of the street, all too conscious that I was toting more money than many New Yorkers earn in a lifetime. At Seventy-Seventh, I turned east and entered the park, darkened but for the weak light coming from a few streetlamps scattered around.

I made my way along an asphalt walking path toward the blue spruce, aware that Saul and Fred were somewhere nearby, which was comforting. I set the case down at the bottom of the spruce and surveyed the area, seeing and hearing nothing except the chirping of crickets and an occasional car horn. As we had agreed upon, I stepped back and began slowly walking away to the east. I had gotten no more than twenty yards from the tree when a voice from the west called out, "You!"

I turned back toward the sound as a shot and a spark of flame came from the direction of the tree. The pain seared me, and I'm sure I must have cried out. I'd been hit and fell to my knees and then, I think, onto my back. I waited for another shot that was sure to come. It did. I braced for the end, but felt nothing. At that moment, everything got fuzzy, and apparently shock set in. I remember hearing Saul shout, and then Fred. From there on, I was in no state to give a narrative, and almost everything I describe from this point until the next day has been supplied by others, including Saul, Fred, Wolfe, and Doc Vollmer. I am not in a position to quarrel with what they reported about my speech or my actions.

They rushed toward me and lifted me upright on wobbly legs. Fred was holding the attaché case, still closed. "The one who shot you, he's a goner," Saul said, motioning to a still, prone figure next to the tree. "Where are you hit?"

"Up there, I think—oh, God, yes." I touched my left shoulder and winced, the dampness from the wound soaking through my windbreaker.

"We'll get you to a hospital—fast," Saul barked.

"No—home!" I said. "Doc Vollmer." I think we three argued, maybe even shouted at one another. But I must have out-yelled Saul and Fred, because I vaguely remember lying on the backseat of the car, with Fred driving and Saul next to him, keeping watch over me. They pulled up in front of the brownstone. "Screw going in the back way," Fred said. "Whoever was after you ain't going to be doing any more shooting now, that's for damned sure."

With one on each side, Fred and Saul got me up the steps to the front door, which was opened by a stunned Fritz. "*Mon Dieu*, Archie!"

I was later told that I was lying on the sofa in the office with Wolfe looking down at me, eyes wide. "Great hounds and Cerberus!" he roared. "What has happened? Saul? Fred?"

"Archie was hit as he walked away after he put the case down next to the tree," Saul said. "We got the money back, and the one who shot him is dead."

I was told that I looked up at the three of them, still dazed. "Okay," I said to Wolfe, "I know you didn't save my life, which means that one of these two guys did. Fred, did you save my bacon again?"

"Not me, Archie, although you know that I would have," Fred said, flustered. "I . . . damn it, I never even had time to get my automatic out. Everything happened so fast."

"So, Saul, it was you. Thank you. I owe you one."

"You don't owe me anything, Archie. Like Fred, I never fired, not once. I had my revolver ready, all right, but before I could pull the trigger, somebody else did, and the man who shot you caught it."

"But who?"

"Good question," Saul said. "But I think right now you should—" He was interrupted by Doc Vollmer, our neighbor and family doctor, who barged into the office. "I came as soon as I got your call, Mr. Wolfe," he panted, carrying his medical bag. "You said it was an emergency, and . . ." He looked down at me. "Archie! *You* are the emergency?"

"He is indeed," Wolfe barked. "He has been shot. And he needs immediate attention."

"A bullet wound?" Vollmer said, running a hand over his long, lean jaw. "You know, of course, that I must report it, Mr. Wolfe."

"It means nothing of the kind, Doctor," Wolfe said. "This is strictly among those of us in this room."

The lanky Vollmer drew himself up to his full height and puffed out his chest. "I am sorry, Mr. Wolfe, but it must be reported."

"No, sir. I seem to remember that over the years, we—and I include Archie—have performed numerous favors for you, including that time when you had found out that you—"

"I remember all too well," the doctor said stiffly, holding up a hand and shaking his head. "All right, where is the wound, Archie?"

"Left shoulder," I said, trying without success to avoid groaning.

"I will need a nurse to help me. Call Carol Francis," Vollmer said to Saul, giving him the number. "She should be home."

"Now, it seems to me your room is the best place to operate," he said to me. "Can you get yourself upstairs?"

"Damned right I can, Doc," I told him. "It's my shoulder, not a leg."

"But you are clearly in pain."

"Yeah, but I can make it. And I sense that you're going to give me something for said pain—or at least I hope so."

As I said earlier, I could give you a play-by-play of the next few hours, but it would be in the words of others, because I don't remember a damned thing. Suffice it to say that Vollmer and his most attractive brunette nurse, Carol, somehow got me fixed up, and they later told me I was given painkillers that sent me on a trip into another world, one in which smiling barefoot maidens with flowing hair and flimsy, transparent gowns hovered over me and stroked my cheeks, feeding me apples and grapes and wine in goblets while playing soft music on golden harps. I recall almost nothing from the time I was shot until nine thirty the next morning, when Fritz knocked gently on my bedroom door and eased in carrying a breakfast tray.

"You do not look the least bit like how I expected a guardian angel to look, but what the hell, you'll do until one comes along," I said.

My feeble attempt at humor did nothing whatever to erase the look of concern on Fritz's face. "Archie, I was so worried when they brought you in last night. Do you think you might be able to eat something?"

"I may have taken a bullet, as apparently happened to me, but it has no appreciable effect on my appetite that I can tell so far. And I like what I'm seeing, and smelling, on that tray. Bring it on."

Never have pork sausage links, scrambled eggs, and cornbread muffins tasted as good as they did that morning, maybe because less than twelve hours earlier on the dank ground of Central Park, it looked like I might not live to see another day.

"Did I get any calls this morning?" I asked.

"None, Archie. I would have told you."

As I ate, Fritz fussed around in the room like a mother hen, sneaking looks at me every so often, maybe to make sure I was still breathing. When he finally took the tray away, I was left with a steaming mug of coffee and a note in an envelope addressed to me. It was from Vollmer, who had surprisingly good handwriting for a doctor. It read:

> *Archie, the bullet has been removed from your left shoulder. It was .38-caliber. It hit your teres minor, a muscle that controls rotation. Fortunately, you are right-handed, so it will cause you less inconvenience than it would for a lefty. The damage is not permanent, and the muscle will heal, albeit slowly. I gave you painkillers last night and left more of them with Fritz, along with instructions on how often they should be ingested. In the next few days, you should begin to do exercises to strengthen the muscle,*

gently at first, and gradually with more vigor. Later today, I will be dropping off a pamphlet outlining those exercises. By now, you will have noticed that your shoulder is tightly wrapped. The dressing will need to be changed in the next few days, probably several times, and I will be sending Miss Francis over to undertake that task. I hardly think you will find her presence to be in any way an inconvenience, but rather the contrary.

Your Neighbor and Friend,
Edwin A. Vollmer, MD

So our grim-faced old sawbones had a sense of humor after all, I thought as I folded the note and returned it to the envelope. I touched my shoulder and found it had indeed been tightly wrapped, and that if I were to take a shower, I would have to cover the dressing with something that was more or less waterproof. Fritz helped there, coming up with a plastic raincoat that we cut up so a sleeve would cover my arm. I then managed to shower, shave, and get myself dressed.

I made my way down to the office at ten forty, which meant Wolfe was still up in the plant rooms, playing with his posies. On my desk, I found a bullet and a note:

A.G.
If you are reading this in the office, I am pleased. It means you are ambulatory, which does not surprise me given your recuperative powers. We will discuss last night's events at eleven if you are able. Also, Doctor Vollmer left the slug that was removed from your shoulder. I trust you are indeed on the mend.

N.W.

The man is all heart, I thought. Fritz came into the office and seemed surprised to see me at my desk. "Archie, should you be up? Is this wise?"

"Our good doctor does not seem to feel I am on death's doorstep, so I might as well behave like someone who has a future. The breakfast you served me was wonderful, as was the coffee, of course. May I have another cup?"

He nodded and left the office as I perused the day's copy of the *Times*, which was on Wolfe's desk along with the morning mail. The pages held no mention of last night's episode in Central Park—probably because it occurred too late to make the home-delivered edition.

I was working on a steaming cup of Fritz's java when Wolfe walked in, placed a raceme of yellow orchids in the vase on his desk, sat, and rang for beer. He dipped his chin in my direction, his version of a greeting, although, unlike his behavior most mornings, he looked long and hard at me, which I took as an expression of concern.

"If you are about to ask me if I slept well, as you usually do, I will answer with a resounding *yes*, although that may well be because I apparently ingested—to use Doc Vollmer's word—something that sent me straight to dreamland."

"Drugs," Wolfe said, pronouncing the word as if it were odious.

"Yeah, I agree. I don't like to take anything I can't spell or pronounce unless it's prepared by Fritz. But at least I'm not hurting like I must have last night, although my memory of recent events is, shall we say, less than reliable."

"Has Miss Hutchinson telephoned this morning?" Wolfe asked.

"No. Fritz would have mentioned it."

He was silent for several seconds, then reached for the *Times*. "Nothing in there about last night," I said. "I already looked."

Wolfe opened the first of two beers Fritz brought in, pouring it into a glass. "Call Mr. Cohen."

"Just what I was thinking." I got Lon on the first ring as Wolfe picked up his receiver.

"What now, Archie? Or are you just lonesome for my voice?"

"I always like to hear your mellifluous voice, oh great scribe and chronicler of Gotham."

"Of course you like to hear me—who wouldn't? I'm one helluvan interesting guy. Now what's on your mind? We have a paper to deliver to our news-hungry readers, as you may recall."

"I am interested in learning about a little episode that transpired in Central Park last night."

"Is that right, Mister Private Detective? Now, just how in Hades do you know about that?"

"Believe it or not, you are not my only pipeline into the goings-on in the City That Never Sleeps."

"If that's the case, why not ask one of your other pipelines about last night?" Lon snapped.

"Oh, come on. After all we've been through together."

"Being in this business, Archie, I am curious by nature—but then, I think you know that."

"Let's say that I do, for purposes of moving the conversation along."

"Good. And just why would I be curious about your interest in what you refer to as 'a little episode' in Central Park?"

"Chalk it up to my also being curious by nature."

"Nice try, Archie," Lon said, "but it won't wash. Does this by chance have anything to do with Cordelia Hutchinson?" I looked at Wolfe, who dipped his chin. Another of his nods.

"It might," I said.

"So! Now we are getting somewhere. Do I sense a scoop?"

"I have no idea—at least not yet. You still haven't told me anything about what happened in the park."

"Why do I have this feeling that you already know at least something about what I am going to say? Well, here goes: Last night about ten or so, shots were fired in the park near the intersection of Central Park West and Seventy-Seventh Street. A passerby who was walking his dog on the sidewalk along Seventy-Seventh told police—and later our reporter—that he had heard what he thought was a gunshot, and then a second one, just to his north in the park. He was pretty rattled, and he said he couldn't see into park that well, given the lighting, but he thought there had been several people moving around, and he could make out at least two figures who were on the ground."

"Interesting."

"Isn't it? The police reported that by the time patrol cars got to the scene—three of them, in fact, along with an ambulance—there was only one guy lying there, and he was quite dead. Shot in the back, and the bullet ruptured his pump. Death was instantaneous."

"Do they know who he was?"

"Yeah, an old friend of the police, so to speak. Noah McManus, a minor-league thug with a record as long as a loan shark's memory. Over the years, he's gotten nailed for armed robbery, burglary, petty larceny, assault with a deadly weapon, and a number of short cons, including—believe it or not—the old shell game, which I thought had become obsolete long ago. One cop who our reporter talked to said McManus was the most inept lawbreaker he had ever seen."

"Well, some old enemy must have finally caught up with him, whatever the reason," I said.

"Could be. McManus seems to have gotten a shot off himself.

A Smith & Wesson .38 Special was found beside his body, with one chamber empty. His prints were on the revolver, which the cops said had been fired recently."

"And you said he was plugged in the back. Odd," I pointed out.

"That's got New York's Finest puzzled, too," Lon said. "If it had been some sort of two-man shootout, wouldn't McManus have caught the bullet in his chest?"

"My point exactly. Anything else?"

"I'm itching to know why you're so curious about this, Archie. Not to mention how you even knew about it in the first place."

I looked over at Wolfe and grinned. "Some day, perhaps, that itch can get itself scratched. Are you going to be playing this big?"

"Are you kidding? Damned right we are. If you recall, some months back, two joggers were mugged in Central Park on separate occasions, and a middle-aged couple from Michigan got held up and robbed here—all three occurrences during the same week. Then the mayor blew a gasket, called a press conference, and ordered the police to step up patrols in the park. 'This is our great city's crown jewel, and we will not have it tarnished as long as I am privileged to hold this office,' he said."

"Which means for you . . . ?"

"Which means we're throwing everything we've got at this. For one thing, the timing is perfect for us as an afternoon paper. The story broke too late for the *Times*, the *Daily News*, and those other morning rags. The *Gazette* that lands on your doorstep shortly will have an eight-column banner reading VIOLENCE AND DEATH IN OUR 'CROWN JEWEL'! We've got the eyewitness account of the dog walker, an interview with our distraught mayor who promises 'immediate action,' and a history of assaults in the park. Oh, and an editorial headlined 'Violence runs amok in a great city.'"

"Mark me down as impressed," I told Lon.

"As well you should be. And by the way, your old pal Inspector Cramer and his thickheaded boss, Commissioner Humbert, were not available for comment."

"You are stretching the definition of *pal*, but I am not at all surprised that both of them are holed up. This will make news across the country."

"And we're there with the first report, which will get picked up by the wire services and distributed before they're able to do their own stories. Now, do you have anything to tell me, anything at all?"

"Sorry, I am of no help."

"Why do I have this feeling that you're holding out on me?"

"Chalk it up to what I call your 'newshound's complex,'" I said. "You guys are so suspicious by nature that you wouldn't believe your dear old grandmother if she told you she loved you."

"My dear old grandmother is long in her grave. Anyway, Archie old pal, being around guys like you for so long has made me leery of taking anything, or anyone, at face value."

"I am truly cut to the quick," I said, trying to sound hurt. "After all we've done for you over these many years, it's enough to make me cry."

"That'll be the day," Lon shot back. "Now if you will excuse me, or even if you won't, we have a paper to put out."

CHAPTER 13

"All right, now what?" I asked Wolfe as we cradled our receivers and I continued to pretend the pain in my shoulder was a figment of my imagination.

"Now you call Miss Hutchinson, of course, and inform her briefly of last night's activities. One would think she must be wondering what transpired."

Wolfe picked up his phone again while I dialed her number. She answered after several rings. "Oh, Archie, how . . . how is everything?" She sounded breathless. "I've been waiting to hear from you. What happened with . . . you know?"

"Do you read any newspapers?" I asked. "Or listen to the radio?"

"No, no, I don't do much of either, I never have. Why do you ask?"

"For one, we still have your money. The individual who was sent to pick it up is dead."

"Dead! How? Who was it?"

"Miss Hutchinson, this is Nero Wolfe. I would like you to

visit us at tonight at six o'clock. Would you find that to be an imposition?"

"No . . . but can't you tell me now what has happened?"

"I would much prefer that we converse face-to-face. Also, as Mr. Goodwin just said, we have your money and wish to return it."

"But what do you mean, what has—"

"I have other business at the moment, but Mr. Goodwin will remain on the line and tell you as much as he deems necessary before your arrival here."

So once again, Wolfe had left me holding the bag, so to speak. I cupped the mouthpiece as I asked, in a near-whisper, "Do you want her to come via the back route again?"

He shook his head and mouthed the words *front door*.

I had difficulty getting rid of Cordelia. She wasn't hysterical, but she was close, repeating the same questions three or four times. I patiently put her off, explaining that some subjects were better discussed in person. That did not persuade her, so I finally had to use a variation on Wolfe's "I have other business" spiel and politely, but firmly, ended the conversation, promising that her questions would be addressed that evening.

"So, am I to gather that we are no longer under a state of siege?" I asked after hanging up.

Wolfe readjusted his bulk and frowned. "I am operating under the assumption that Mr. McManus was the individual commissioned to end your life. Do you agree?"

"That thought certainly had occurred to me," I said, "although it is possible that more than one person has it in for yours truly."

"No doubt given our occupation, others might wish to exact retribution against you. But murder I find to be highly unlikely in more than one situation. However, you are the individual who has been targeted—and wounded—and I would not presume to advise you as to how to protect yourself."

"I've gotten this far in life, and I'm still upright and above ground; I'll take my chances. Right now, I'm damned tired of sneaking out the back way like some guy hastily dashing out of a woman's bedroom as her husband comes in the front door. You are the one who has the brains in this operation, as you are so often eager to point out. Do you have any idea who might have commissioned McManus to dispatch me?"

"Not at the moment," Wolfe said as he picked up his current book.

"Do you have any special instructions regarding Miss Hutchinson's visit?" I asked.

"None," he said. "Let us hope she is happy to be reunited with her money."

At five minutes to six, the doorbell rang. I was pleased that Cordelia, our maybe-client, was on time, although I was not surprised. I swung open the door and gave her an exaggerated bow, just because I felt like it.

She stood on the stoop as if she were riveted to the spot, her eyes unblinking. "Archie, what has happened?"

"We will give you a report. Please come in."

She gingerly—I don't what else to call it—stepped across the threshold and into the front hall, clutching her purse as if it might suddenly fly out of her grip. With a gentle hand on her elbow, I steered her toward the office, although she seemed reluctant to move ahead.

"As you can see, Mr. Wolfe is not here yet. Can I get you something to drink? Coffee, tea, or maybe a glass of wine? Our selection is very good," I said as I motioned her toward the red leather chair.

"No, thank you . . . No." Cordelia sat and stared up at me as though I didn't look right to her.

"I did shave this morning, didn't I?" I asked as I ran a hand across my cheek. "And I hope I washed behind the ears. And I also hope that I remembered to properly knot my tie."

Cordelia blushed. "I'm sorry, I'm still . . ." Her unfinished sentence hung in the air.

"Ah, of course. You have to still be stunned about everything that happened last night."

She opened her mouth to reply but stopped as Wolfe stepped into the room. "Miss Hutchinson," he said, moving behind his desk, sitting, and ringing for beer. "I trust Mr. Goodwin offered you refreshments."

"Yes, he did. Nothing for me, thank you." She still seemed trancelike.

Wolfe considered her. "How much do you know about the events of last night in Central Park?"

"Very little," she said, shifting in the chair, "except that Archie told me someone was killed and that you still have the money."

"To say the least, the operation did not go as planned," Wolfe replied as he opened the first of two beers Fritz placed before him and poured it into a pilsner glass, watching the foam settle. "Mr. Goodwin delivered the valise with the money to the base of a specific tree, per the instructions you received. As he walked away, he was shot in the shoulder and fell."

"Oh, oh! How awful!"

"Let me continue, please. The man who shot Mr. Goodwin was then shot—fatally, by an unknown gunman. The body has been identified as that of Noah McManus, who had an extensive criminal record. Does that name have any significance to you?"

"No, should it?" Cordelia asked.

Wolfe raised his shoulders and let them drop. "Not necessarily, although it seems apparent that he was sent by the blackmailer to retrieve the money. Unless, of course, he *was* the blackmailer."

"His name means absolutely nothing to me," Cordelia stressed.

"Just so. This brings us to the money, which we will return to you. Archie, please."

I went to the safe and pulled out the attaché case, laying it on my desk and opening it.

"Miss Hutchinson, I invite you to count the currency and verify that it all is there," Wolfe said.

She got up and eyed the bundles of dough in the case. "I don't feel that is necessary," she said. "I trust you both."

"I insist," Wolfe said. "Sit at Mr. Goodwin's desk. This will take a while."

Cordelia reluctantly parked in my chair and began the count while I wandered out to the kitchen for a glass of milk and to watch Fritz finish preparations for dinner: lobster in white wine sauce with tarragon, along with a celery and cantaloupe salad.

By the time I sauntered back to the office, our guest had just finished her audit. "It is all here," she said to Wolfe.

He nodded, if you consider his slight dip of a chin as a nod. "Archie, type out a receipt for Miss Hutchinson to sign. Word it thusly: 'Received from Nero Wolfe, seventy-five thousand dollars in cash.'"

"Is this really necessary?" she asked as she vacated my chair and moved over to the red leather one. "I said before that I trust you."

"Nonetheless, we must maintain a businesslike relationship," Wolfe replied.

"But I feel guilty. I have still never paid you anything, Mr. Wolfe."

"Would you be more comfortable if I asked for one thousand dollars?"

"Yes, yes I would," she said, pulling out a checkbook and

starting to write. "But what about the blackmail? Will you continue to represent me? I can give you a retainer, and knowing your reputation, I am sure it should be for far more than a thousand dollars."

"No, the amount I quoted will be sufficient for now," Wolfe said. "Do you feel that after last night's events, the blackmailer will continue to beset you?"

Cordelia shook her head. "I . . . just don't know. I can't say."

"Let us see what, if anything, develops in the next few days, Miss Hutchinson. For now, Mr. Goodwin will escort you home in a taxi. You should not be venturing forth alone with that amount of money in your possession."

As usual, Wolfe had volunteered me for a task without bothering to inform me in advance. This would, of course, mean my having a late dinner in the kitchen, since Wolfe does not delay his own dining for anything less than an earthquake—which New York rarely, if ever, gets—or a power failure. Now that I think of it, we once did have the lights go out in the middle of dinner, and on that occasion, the lord and master of the house simply had Fritz bring a candelabra into the dining room.

CHAPTER 14

Once we and the oh-so-precious attaché case were inside a cab and headed north, Cordelia leaned over, put a hand on my arm, and whispered, "I am so glad that you were not hurt badly, Archie."

"We are in definite agreement on that," I said. "Do you have any further thoughts about what happened in the park?"

She pulled away and stiffened. "Of course not. As I said in your office, I don't know what to make of it all."

We rode the rest of the way to Sutton Place in silence. For those unfamiliar with Manhattan geography, Sutton, a short, north-and-south thoroughfare on the Upper East Side, has long been a symbol of affluence and a home to the famous and fortunate. When someone in town becomes highly successful, Lon Cohen is fond of saying, "He just punched his ticket to Sutton Place."

The cab pulled up to the Hutchinsons' co-op building, a ten-story brick fortress fronted by an arched green canopy. The entrance was protected by a tall doorman clad in an elaborate blue-and-gold uniform only slightly more elegant than those worn by the guardsmen who wow tourists daily at Buckingham Palace. He actually saluted as we climbed out of the taxi.

"Evening, Miss Hutchinson," he said.

"Good evening, Brewster. Nice weather we're having, isn't it?"

He nodded smartly, saluting again, as I handed Cordelia the case full of lettuce. We said our brief good-byes, and I climbed into the Yellow Cab.

Back in the kitchen of the brownstone, I ate lobster from a heated plate as Fritz fussed over me.

"How are you feeling, Archie?" he asked, his face full of concern.

"Contrary to anything you may have heard, the patient will survive," I told him between bites. "And the best medicine, far and away, is your skill with a skillet and a stove and an oven and . . . I could go on and on, but you get the idea. You are a miracle worker."

He blushed but followed it with a frown. "You are using the front door again. Is that safe?"

"Mr. Wolfe and I believe so," I half-lied. "There is some dessert left, isn't there? Or did our employer eat it all?"

That got a smile, a broad one. He turned to a cabinet and pulled out a plate holding a fat wedge of blueberry pie, baked earlier that day. "You would like ice cream with it?" he asked.

"Just how long have you known me, Fritz?" I didn't wait for his answer, handing the pie back to him so that he could do the à la mode number on it with his ice cream scoop.

When I got to the office with a cup of coffee, Wolfe was seated at his desk reading his latest book, *The Struggle for Europe* by Chester Wilmot. I parked at my desk and pivoted to face him.

He dog-eared a page, closed the book, and set it on his blotter. "The young lady and the money were returned home without event." It wasn't a question.

"Of course. With me on the case, could you expect anything less?"

When he didn't answer, I added, "The young lady was hardly chatty during our ride up to that famous street paved with gold."

"This is an interesting time for Miss Hutchinson," Wolfe remarked, "and it may become more interesting."

"Meaning?"

"She has a great deal to think about at the moment. It will be instructive to learn where those thoughts lead her."

"That's cryptic."

"It was not meant to be. How are you feeling?"

"A little sore here, a little sore there. I try not to think about it. But since you asked, I'm more tired than is usually the case at this hour. It's time for me to turn in."

Wolfe nodded and returned to his book.

The next morning, I finished breakfast and had just settled in at my desk with coffee when the phone jangled. I gave my usual "Nero Wolfe's office, Archie Goodwin speaking."

"Goodwin? Oh yeah, you're Wolfe's dogsbody, aren't you?" a gruff voice asked.

"I need to know the definition of that word before answering," I told him, "but for the record, I do happen to be in the employ of Nero Wolfe."

"Well listen, Goodwin, this is Parkhurst Hutchinson. That name mean anything to you?"

"I'm not sure that I have heard it before."

"Huh. So you say, but I don't believe you for a second. I am in the newspapers all the time. You may see it if you happen to read the business pages. And my daughter just happens to be a client of your boss."

"I'm sorry, Mr. Hutchinson, but I am not able to discuss or

even identify any clients without Mr. Wolfe's permission. And he is not likely to discuss them, either, although I cannot speak for him."

"Oh, cut the crap, Goodwin. This is my daughter I'm talking about, and I want to see Wolfe—today!"

"Mr. Wolfe is otherwise occupied at the moment, but I will relay the message to him."

"You had damned well better, ace. And while you're at it, stop trying to sound like Jeeves. I want to hear from him this morning, or by God, I will be banging on your door until it comes off its hinges. I realize he doesn't leave his home on business, but I know where the fat man lives."

He gave me a telephone number. I started to reply, but the line went dead. I began to dial up Wolfe in the greenhouse on the roof, where he and Theodore Horstmann were nurturing one of the world's greatest collections of orchids as usual, but I had bothered him during his greenhouse time very recently and chose not to do it again. Besides, I was so put off by Parkhurst Hutchinson and his use of *dogsbody* and *ace* that, as far as I was concerned, he could wait forever to hear from Nero Wolfe. And I didn't understand the Jeeves reference, but I had a pretty good idea it was meant as an insult.

When Wolfe came down from the plant rooms at eleven and rang for beer, I waited until he got himself settled. "Care to guess who called this morning?" I asked with a grin.

Knowing how much he hates guessing games, I was not surprised when he made a face.

"Parkhurst Hutchinson. Does that name mean anything to you?" I said, repeating the question I had gotten from our angry caller.

I was rewarded with a glower. "Of course it does. Report."

"Mr. Hutchinson wants to see you—today. He says he's ready to tear our front door clean off its hinges."

Wolfe raised his eyebrows. "Is he indeed?"

I gave him the rest of our mercifully brief conversation. "He must think you have been abusing his youngest daughter. I'll call back and tell him to push a boulder up a mountain."

"Pfui. Telephone the man and tell him to be here at nine."

"Do I at least have permission to be rude to him on the phone?"

"You do not. The way I may react in his presence is a different matter."

I picked up my phone and dialed the number Hutchinson gave me earlier. A businesslike female voice told me I had reached "The Great Eastern and Pacific Railway System." When she asked with whom I wished to speak, I gave Hutchinson's name, then mine, telling her I was returning his call. I nodded to Wolfe to pick up his receiver.

"Ah, Goodwin, the loyal dogsbody. Hah! I figured that I would be hearing from you," Hutchinson snorted. "Did you get me set up with your boss for today?"

"Mr. Hutchinson, this is Nero Wolfe. I expect you to be here at nine tonight, and alone."

"Sorry, Mr. Wolfe, I will be at the annual banquet of the National Railroad Executives Association at the Churchill Hotel, which figures to last until at least eleven. I will come at five this afternoon, period."

"Sir, I will not be available at that hour. If you insist on seeing me, it is nine o'clock or not at all, period."

"Who the hell do you think you are?"

"I know very well who I am. If you wish to see me, it will be on my terms and in my office."

Hutchinson let loose with a few words not worth repeating,

then took what sounded like a deep breath. "Do you treat everybody this way?" he demanded.

"Only when I am faced with an ultimatum," Wolfe said.

Another deep breath. "All right, nine it is, but by God, you had better come up with some answers for me."

"That depends entirely upon the questions you ask, sir."

Hutchinson swore again, then hung up.

"Sure you want to invite this guy into our house?" I said.

"We have hosted worse," Wolfe replied, turning to his beer.

A few minutes before nine that night, I restocked the drink cart in the office. I had told Wolfe that, based on two brief phone conversations, Hutchinson didn't seem like someone we should waste good alcohol on, but he pointed out, as he had numerous times, that "a guest is a jewel on the cushion of hospitality."

"Some jewel," I grumped.

The front doorbell chimed at nine sharp. As viewed through the one-way glass in the front door, Parkhurst Hutchinson looked like I expected him to: medium height, stocky, well dressed in a double-breasted three-piece suit, and wearing a homburg atop his head and a surly expression on his round, ruddy face.

"Yes?" I said, swinging the door open. "Can I help you?"

"Cut the comedy," he rasped. "You know who I am and why I'm here."

"I normally ask for some type of identification before I let anyone in, but you look harmless enough. Step across the threshold."

Hutchinson shot me a glare that would have wilted a lesser man, but I merely smiled and took his hat as he entered, hanging it on the coat rack in the hall. "Follow me," I ordered, leading him to the office and directing him to the red leather chair.

"Where's Wolfe?" he barked as he sat.

"He will be along shortly. Can I get you something to drink?

We have a good scotch, a good rye, a good gin, and a good almost-anything-else-you-could-possibly-want."

"I don't need anything, dammit, and—oh, what the hell, I'll have a scotch on the rocks," Hutchinson said.

I poured and handed him the drink. As he was taking a sip, Wolfe strode in, having waited in the kitchen until I pressed the buzzer under his center desk drawer, which is also the buzzer he normally uses to call for beer.

"Good evening, sir," Wolfe said as he detoured around his desk and sat. "I see Mr. Goodwin already has provided you with refreshments. I am about to have beer myself."

"I did not come here to socialize," Hutchinson said, sticking out the uppermost of his double chins. "I want to talk to you about my daughter."

"Really?" Wolfe purred. "Do I know your daughter?"

"Don't try playing your hotshot detective games with me, Wolfe," Hutchinson said with a snarl. "I know all about you and how you bilk your clients. I've had you investigated. I'm on to you."

"It is good to know you have done your homework, sir," Wolfe said as Fritz brought in beer and set it on the desk. "It saves time on introductions."

"And whether you know a lot about me or not, you must be aware of my name, which is in the papers all the time. I am Parkhurst Hutchinson, as I am sure you know, although my friends call me Park."

"I prefer Mr. Hutchinson," Wolfe said dryly. If the railroad tycoon took that as an insult, he did not show it.

"All right, let's get down to business," Hutchinson said. "I'm here on a very serious matter."

"As is everyone who sits in that chair."

"Don't try to play this down. It's my youngest daughter we're talking about, dammit. I want to know why she is seeing you. And don't try to deny it. Cordelia's been acting strangely of late, and I got our maid, who Cordelia confides in, to admit that she has visited you. I had to squeeze it out of her by threatening to fire her. If that shocks you, too bad. That's how I have to operate to get things done sometimes." Hutchinson sat back in the chair, folding his arms across his chest and smirking.

"How old is your daughter?" Wolfe asked.

"Twenty-four. What of it?"

"She is well into her majority. I suggest you ask her yourself to discuss her actions with you."

"She may be twenty-four chronologically, but emotionally and in other ways, she's more like a teenager," Hutchinson huffed, "and I sure as hell don't want people like you taking advantage of her innocence."

Wolfe drank beer and set the glass down, dabbing his lips with a handkerchief. "So you have no idea why she might want to use the services of an investigator?"

"I asked her, but she just clammed up on me," Hutchinson said, now sounding less cocky.

"If your daughter does not choose to share her concerns with you, I can only offer my sympathy," Wolfe said.

"So you do not deny she has hired you?"

"I neither admit nor deny it, sir. Nor do I see any reason to justify my actions to you."

"What if I was to hire you?"

Wolfe looked surprised. "For what purpose?"

"To, uh, help my daughter with whatever her problem is. The maid also told me that Cordelia feels very comfortable with your man here." Hutchinson shot a glance in my direction.

"So you are suggesting that I would in effect function as a spy, reporting to you about your daughter's activities."

"I would not put it that way," the railroad millionaire said, trying without success to act offended. I found it hard to believe he was ever offended.

"A rose by any other name. I am sorry, sir, but I am not for sale," Wolfe told him. "And moments ago, you expressed concern about 'people like me' taking advantage of your daughter's innocence. I can see no further benefit to either of us in continuing this conversation."

"That's a damned high-handed attitude you've got, Wolfe!" Hutchinson rasped, standing and turning toward the doorway.

Wolfe watched without reaction as the enraged man stomped out and down the hall with me in his wake. Before I could reach his homburg, he plucked it off the rack and opened the front door. He would have slammed it behind him if I hadn't stopped it in mid-arc. He hurried down the seven steps to the street and climbed into the backseat of a burgundy Lincoln limousine idling at the curb. The uniformed chauffeur pulled away smoothly as I waved, but because it was dark, I don't know if the gesture got returned.

When I got back to the office, Wolfe was signing the letters I had typed earlier. "Well, you may have just missed a chance at one dandy payday," I said.

"How would you have felt if I had accepted Mr. Hutchinson's offer?"

"Lousy."

"Not the word I would have chosen, but it suffices," he said. "However, I feel confident that we have not seen the last of Mr. Hutchinson."

"Really? Do you care to expound on that?"

"I do not," he said, turning back to his correspondence.

CHAPTER 15

The next morning, I had just settled myself in the office when the telephone rang. Not a good sign as of late. I had begun toying with the idea of not answering before at least ten a.m., and telling Fritz to likewise let it ring. Trouble seems to come early. It did again.

"Hello, Archie, old pal." It was the unmistakable voice of Lon Cohen of the *Gazette.*

"It's the 'old pal' part of that greeting that makes me nervous," I said. "Do I owe you money?"

"Don't I wish! You may recall that you were the big winner at poker the other night. No, this has to do with someone from your past. And by the way, just the other day you called me 'old pal.' I was simply returning the friendly salutation."

"Thanks so much. Now, who is this from my past? Please don't keep me in suspense—let's have it."

"I know you recall Alan Marx, whose brother Wolfe helped send to Sing Sing's high-voltage chair some years back."

"Of course I remember him," I said, my heart pumping furiously. I was not about to tell Lon that Marx had been on Wolfe's and my mind lately. "What's he done?"

"It's what's been done to him. He was found in his luxury condo in the East Eighties this morning, deader than the Knicks' playoff chances this season."

"Huh? Natural causes?"

"Well . . . no, which makes for a great story, at least for those of us who live for that sort of thing. A maid came in this morning around seven to clean, as she usually does, and she found Mr. Marx sprawled on the living room floor next to the fireplace with one side of his head caved it.

"Seems he apparently was coshed by a poker that was found lying beside him. We just got the police reports, and of course I recalled his connection to you and Wolfe. Alan Marx was outspoken about detesting both of you."

"Outspoken is an understatement, given the names he called us—particularly Wolfe—at the time. How well I remember," I said. "Mr. Marx must have had other enemies, though."

"So it would now seem," Lon said. "However, I felt I should let you know that Inspector Cramer may just stop by the brownstone. You know how he likes to connect the dots, whether or not they make any sense."

"I will alert Mr. Wolfe. Any other information?"

"That's all we've got here at the moment."

"Thanks for the heads-up."

"Always happy to be of help. And who knows, before this is over, maybe you will have something of interest for yours truly."

"You mean our 'old pal'?"

"That's me. We're going to play this big, given that Marx had a lot of visibility around town—fine art collector, patron of the opera, the symphony, the ballet, etcetera, etcetera."

"I won't forget those etceteras, old pal," I said. "Now get back to putting out the paper. Aren't you on a deadline? That's how you usually brush me off."

"Thanks for reminding me. Gotta go."

When Wolfe came down from the plant rooms at eleven, I told him we might be getting a visit from Cramer.

He glowered. "Why?"

I told him about Lon's call, and he glowered some more, then sighed. "Confound it. If he comes, tell him I am not here."

"But he knows you are always here," I argued. "And if you were to hide in the kitchen, or the plant rooms, or your bedroom, then I would have to deal with him alone. I am not paid well enough to perform that kind of service, although this might be a good time to discuss a raise."

That warranted yet another glower. "Relate everything Mr. Cohen said."

"It's pretty skimpy," I said, repeating our conversation word for word.

"Skimpy indeed," Wolfe remarked. "You should have questioned him more thoroughly."

"Just a minute. Bear in mind that when we talked, the discovery of Marx's body had occurred just two hours earlier. I think I got everything that Lon and the *Gazette* had at the time."

He grunted, which can mean any number of things, from dissatisfaction with my performance to his unhappiness over having to go to work. As I have often said, Nero Wolfe is lazy—brilliant but lazy. He knows this, which is one of the reasons he keeps me around. Among my functions is the task to be a burr under his saddle, a prod to get him going.

Wolfe barely had time to sample the first of his two pre-luncheon beers when the doorbell chimed. I looked at my watch, which read eleven-twenty. "That will be Cramer. Do I let the man enter or make him keep pushing the button until he gets a blister on his finger?"

His answer was a frown and a shrug, so I headed down the hall. "Good morning, Inspector," I said, throwing open the door. "Is this a social call?"

"Just when has it ever been a social call?" Cramer grumped, handing me his battered fedora and marching by me. By the time I got to the office, he was already planted in the red leather chair like he owned it, his eyes fixed on Wolfe, who looked up from his book.

"Sorry to interrupt your reading," the inspector said.

"It is not the first time," Wolfe said, "and it likely will not be the last."

"Don't be too sure of that. As I know you are aware, the heat is on, and at least one very large and self-important local newspaper has suggested in an editorial that it is time for me to seriously consider retiring. To be precise, they wrote that 'Cramer's time is long past.'"

"All because of the Central Park murder?"

"That's for starters, and now we've got another killing, which is why I am here. Of all people, you of course remember Alan Marx."

"He is hard to forget," Wolfe replied.

"Marx was found murdered in his pricey Upper East Side abode last night, but maybe you already know that." Wolfe made no response.

"Somebody had bashed in his skull, apparently with a heavy poker from the fireplace," Cramer continued. "It happened sometime before midnight, or so we've been told. His wife was out of town visiting relatives in Pennsylvania, and none of the neighbors heard anything—not surprising given that the walls in that building are unusually thick. And the doorman said he didn't see anybody come in asking for Marx. The rub here is that according to residents of the building, the doorman has a reputation for dozing at his desk in the entrance hall. So almost anyone could have walked through that entrance hall, ridden up in the self-service elevator, and gotten as far as Marx's door."

"Mr. Marx must have let the individual in," Wolfe observed.

"Precisely. The man knew his killer. I find that most interesting."

"What is your point, Mr. Cramer?"

"Bear with me. I am getting to it, in my own slow and simple way. Here is something else that I find interesting: Goodwin here is shot at as he's about to enter the brownstone. Then soon afterward, your building itself gets fired on. And now, a man who has for years made public his hatred of Nero Wolfe is found murdered. I am not a big believer in coincidences, maybe because all these years on the job have made a skeptic of me."

"Continue."

As is his practice when in Wolfe's office, Cramer took a cigar from his breast pocket and jammed it into his mouth, unlit. "Had you heard from Alan Marx recently?" he asked.

"I have not," Wolfe said. "Archie?"

"No, sir, not a word."

Cramer turned to me. "And you have not had occasion to visit Marx's residence?"

"I wasn't even aware of where he lived, Inspector. Honest."

"Do you feel okay?" the inspector posed.

"Sure, why?"

"You seemed to be a little bit stiff, the way you walked when I came in, kind of lopsided."

"I did something to my shoulder when I was exercising the other day, nothing major, but thanks for asking."

"Are you quite finished?" Wolfe asked our guest.

"You understand that I had to go through the motions," Cramer said in a tone that, for him, was conciliatory. "Sooner or later, you can bet that Commissioner Humbert would have asked me if I had brought up the subject with you."

"And now you can tell him you have," Wolfe said. "Is there anything else?"

"Not at the moment. I'm up to my eyeballs fighting a two-front battle, with the shooting of a thug in our city's showcase park on the one hand and the murder of a prominent patron of the arts on the other. If I don't see the two of you again, I am sure you will not miss my visits." He rose, put the cigar back in his pocket, and ambled off without another word.

"Not the same old Cramer," I said when I had returned to the office after seeing him out. "When I handed him his hat, he actually said, 'Thanks, Archie.' I almost keeled over from the shock."

"Mr. Cramer feels very sorry for himself at the moment," Wolfe said. "And not without some justification. The inspector finds himself waging war on two fronts, as he said, and either of the incidents alone would be a large headache for the police department, given the circumstances. Together, they constitute a migraine of epic proportions."

"Okay, so much for the mess Cramer finds himself in, but after all, that comes with the job," I said. "That's what he gets paid for. What are your thoughts about Marx's murder?"

"I have none at the moment. It is possible his acerbic nature—with which we are all too familiar—has inflamed someone in the arts community to the point where violence ensued. Based on what I have seen, the artistic temperament manifests itself in unpredictable and occasionally violent ways."

"That is not very helpful," I told him. "Do you think Marx was our phantom telephone man? Neither of us ever heard him speak, so we wouldn't have recognized his voice. We have had no calls for several days now. I almost miss getting them—but not quite."

"It is possible," Wolfe said, "although I am not yet ready to state with certainty that we have gotten the last of those calls."

CHAPTER 16

Two days passed in which we did not hear either from our phantom caller or from Cordelia. But on the third morning, a surprising call came. I was in the office alone, entering orchid germination records, when I answered the phone.

"Mr. Goodwin, this is Parkhurst Hutchinson." Based on the voice alone, it was hard to believe this was the same bullying, blustering man who had stormed in and stormed out of the office so recently. He spoke in a voice only a couple of levels above a whisper.

"What can I do for you?" I asked in my we-don't-need-any-of-whatever-you're-selling tone.

"I don't blame you for wanting to hang up on me. I behaved poorly the other day, and for that I am sorry. I want to make an appointment to see Mr. Wolfe—along with my daughter."

"And for what purpose?" I snapped, still angry about having been called a dogsbody, a word I now knew the meaning of. I now also understood his Jeeves reference.

Parkhurst continued: "She and I wish to hire Mr. Wolfe to get to the bottom of this ugly blackmailing business."

"I cannot speak for Mr. Wolfe, but I will discuss the matter with him later this morning."

"I—we—are willing to pay whatever he charges," Hutchinson said, still sounding like a chagrined schoolboy.

"I will pass that information along to Mr. Wolfe."

"Will you call me when he has made a decision? We can come to see him whenever it is convenient for him."

I asked for the best number to reach him and said it was likely, but by no means definite, that we would get back to him later in the day.

When Wolfe came down at eleven and got himself firmly planted in the only chair in which he is truly comfortable, I swiveled to face him. "Well, you have done it again," I said.

"Indeed?"

"Indeed is right. As you predicted, we got a call this morning from his eminence Parkhurst Hutchinson."

"He was chagrined about his earlier behavior and now desires to hire us," Wolfe stated as he rang for beer.

"Correct again, oh great reader of minds, although he seeks to become a client in tandem with his daughter. They want to see you together, at any time you specify. It could be a nice payday."

"You are now singing a far different song than you were after Mr. Hutchinson left here. When I asked how you would feel about having him as a client, you said 'lousy.'"

"We may have on our hands the 'new and improved' version of the man, to use words normally associated with products that are being advertised."

"Perhaps. Call Mr. Hutchinson and tell him and his daughter to be here at nine tonight."

As my boss sampled his first beer of the day, I dialed Hutchinson, who picked up before the first ring had ended. "Mr. Wolfe will see you and Cordelia here at nine. Be prompt. Mr. Wolfe has an extremely busy schedule."

"Oh, we will, Mr. Goodwin, you can be sure of it. Thank you, and please thank Mr. Wolfe."

After I hung up, Wolfe paused between sips of beer and said, "You seem to have abandoned your usual cordiality."

"Okay, so I hereby admit that Hutchinson brings out the worst in me. 'Dogsbody' my foot."

"I agree the gentleman is not always tactful. But you already have sensed a change in his demeanor. We will see tonight whether that change can survive our discussion."

At eight fifty-five, the bell rang. I opened the door to Mr. Hutchinson and his daughter, both of whom smiled and stepped in. He seemed meek and she seemed meeker as I walked them down the hall to the office, where I gave him the red leather chair and her one of the yellow ones. "Mr. Wolfe will be with you shortly," I said. "Can I get you something to drink?" I asked, motioning to the bar cart against one wall. "As you already know," I said to Hutchinson, "we have everything from scotch and rye to beer and wine."

"I believe I will have a scotch on the rocks," he said, nodding. "What about you, honey?"

Cordelia looked up at me, down at her lap, then up again. "Would you have a dry sherry, by any chance?"

"I would, and it is a good one," I told her, going to the bar. After I had served them, Wolfe walked in, nodded, sat, and rang for beer. "Good evening. I see you have refreshments. Let us begin."

"Before we do," Hutchinson said, holding up a fleshy hand, "I want to apologize for my behavior here on my previous visit. I can only say, in my defense, that I was terribly worried about

Cordelia." He reached over and squeezed his daughter's hand. "Since then, she and I have had some long and very meaningful father-daughter talks, and I have come to realize the terrible pressures she has been under." As he talked, Cordelia said nothing, nodding once or twice and studying her hands in her lap.

"She told me everything," Hutchinson continued, "including her understanding of that gun battle in Central Park, in which I understand Mr. Goodwin was wounded." He looked at me with what I took to be a sympathetic expression. "She also opened up to us about her . . . minor indiscretion in Italy," Hutchinson continued, "and both her mother and I let her know that we support her one hundred percent. As for whomever it is that's blackmailing her, we want him stopped."

"What prevents you from going to the police?" Wolfe asked.

"We desire to avoid the publicity, don't we, darling?" he said. Cordelia nodded, still silent and looking as if she would rather be almost anywhere but here.

"As you may know, my daughter is engaged to a fine young man, Lance Mercer, and she understandably does not want anything to jeopardize their relationship. Even though she did nothing that I consider in any way sinful in Florence, appearances can be damning, including that photograph she showed to her mother and me yesterday. We are hoping that you can find and stop this evil man, and do so as quietly as possible."

"If I agree to accept this commission, it must be upon my terms and without reservation," Wolfe said.

"I understand," Hutchinson said.

"No, sir, I do not believe you do. My agents and I, including Mr. Goodwin, must be free to meet with anyone remotely connected with your daughter. That includes her siblings and her friends."

"Oh, no!" Cordelia yelped, suddenly coming alive.

"That is my proviso," Wolfe said. "Without it, I cannot be expected to conduct an effective investigation."

"But, you don't have to talk to Lanny, do you?" Cordelia said, sniffling and beginning to tear up.

"We will try to avoid meeting with him," Wolfe said, turning to me. "How do you feel about that, Archie?"

"I believe we can work around the young man," I said.

"And must my brothers and sisters know why I am being blackmailed?"

"Mr. Goodwin is a skilled interviewer," Wolfe said. "When necessary, he can be the very soul of discretion. He will make every effort to avoid specifics."

I nodded my assent.

"Before we go any further, you need to understand that there is always the possibility we might uncover information you find distasteful, unpleasant, and embarrassing to you and your family," Wolfe said.

"I'm not sure I follow you," Hutchinson replied, frowning.

"I am being candid, and I assume you want candor in anyone you hire. You must be prepared for whatever we uncover."

The tycoon sighed. "We'll take our chances, won't we, honey?"

Cordelia nodded, biting a lip.

"Before we conclude, I need something else from you, sir," Wolfe added. "Without prior warning, Mr. Goodwin may find it difficult to talk to your offspring. You can pave the way for him by explaining to them that your daughter has been threatened—you need not get more specific than that—and that you have hired an investigator in hopes of unearthing the miscreant, and that the investigator may wish to speak to them."

"Oh, but they might think they are somehow being accused," Cordelia said.

"Not necessarily," Wolfe said. "Mr. Goodwin can say he is

interviewing everyone who knows you in hopes that one or more of them may have an idea as to who might seek to harm or intimidate you."

"I believe that is a legitimate approach," Hutchinson said to his daughter. "These men have had a lot of experience in a world we know nothing of. I will take it upon myself to call your brothers and sisters." He turned to Wolfe. "We will pay whatever you charge."

"That will depend on how the investigation progresses," Wolfe said, "but I can assure you my fee will be no less than fifty thousand dollars, plus expenses. And based upon what I know and anticipate, some of those expenses may run to a considerable amount."

Neither father nor daughter flinched at the figure, and why should they? I thought. I felt Wolfe was letting them off easy.

"Would you like a check now?" Hutchinson asked.

"For half the amount," Wolfe said, "with the other half, plus the expenses due, on completion of the assignment."

America's most famous railroad executive smoothly drew an alligator-skin checkbook and a gold fountain pen from his breast pocket and wrote out a check to America's most famous private investigator, placing it on the corner of Wolfe's desk. "I assure you the money is in my account," he said. "Do you need to ask questions of either of us now?"

"I think not," Wolfe said. "Mr. Goodwin will need to get addresses and numbers of all those we feel it necessary to talk to. That can be done by telephone in the morning."

"Why wait?" Hutchinson said. "We can do that right now. We are anxious to have you start in."

"Just so," Wolfe remarked. "I regret that I have another engagement, but you may stay right here and supply Mr. Goodwin with everything he needs."

With that, he rose, tugged down the points on his vest, and strode out of the room to that other engagement, which I knew to be in the kitchen. We had not consumed all of the shrimp bordelaise Fritz served for dinner, and Wolfe would see to it that there were no leftovers.

I refreshed Hutchinson's drink, but Cordelia said no to a refill of the sherry. The father was much more forthcoming with supplying information than his daughter. She bridled when I asked her how to reach her friend Marlene Peters. "I really don't see why you would need to talk to her," she said plaintively.

"Pumpkin, we need to trust Mr. Goodwin and Mr. Wolfe on this," her father said softly, reaching over and squeezing her shoulder. "Didn't you tell us a while back that Marlene's back in town, and that you had lunch with her? After all, she is probably your best friend and would want what's in your best interests. You will have to call her and give her a reason a detective needs to talk to her. It wouldn't make any sense for me to telephone her."

Cordelia nodded, sighed, and pulled an address book out of her purse. She read off a phone number and an address on the Lower East Side, along with the number of the bookstore where Marlene worked. She even gave me the particulars on how to reach Lance Mercer, though more reluctantly. I tried to assuage her concern by stressing that I would make every effort to avoid talking to him.

Hutchinson himself rattled off the information on Cordelia's siblings, although when he came to the ne'er-do-well son, Doug, he tightened up noticeably. Apparently, the rift was still there.

I thanked them both for their help and said Wolfe and I would keep them apprised as to our progress. As I escorted them to the front door, Hutchinson seemed bent on playing the role of the hail-fellow-well-met, perhaps to make up for his earlier behavior. Cordelia, on the other hand, seemed even more withdrawn than when they had arrived, which I ascribed to her fear that somehow our investigation would complicate her future with one Lance Mercer.

After the pair rode away in the chauffeur-driven Lincoln that had been purring at our curb during their visit, I headed into the kitchen for a late evening snack. There were several possibilities, but sadly, shrimp bordelaise was not one of them.

CHAPTER 17

In case you are wondering, I had not forgotten about the caller who wanted to terminate me. Although I initially saw no apparent connection between Noah McManus and the Hutchinson project, I now had to question whether McManus, the Central Park gunman who came very close to finishing me off moments before his own death, could have been my nemesis all along. Or was he prepared to shoot anyone who delivered the briefcase full of money?

I knew how to learn something more about the man, which is why I gave Saul Panzer an assignment. Saul is not only the best freelance private operative on the planet, he also has a wealth of connections—some of them persons of what might be termed "questionable repute."

"Can you find out for me if the late and unlamented Mr. McManus had any sort of accent?" I had asked him. "Maybe an Irish brogue or a Scottish burr or a Southern drawl?" Any of those speech patterns would have eliminated him as my vexer.

Saul called me the next morning and quickly eliminated the

petty hoodlum from consideration all right, but not in a way I expected. “Archie, I got hold of a joe who knew your man, seems they used to hang out in the same pool hall. He tells me McManus had the worst stutter he had ever seen, claimed the guy couldn’t spit out five words in a row or complete a single sentence without stammering.” So much for McManus being my telephone pal, so presumably “the voice,” as I had come to call him, was still at large.

But at the moment, I had other concerns: setting up meetings with members of the Hutchinson family and with Marlene Peters.

For no particular reason, my first call was to Cordelia’s eldest sibling, Annie, who worked as an advertising copywriter for one of the big agencies on Madison Avenue. The switchboard operator put me through to her, and she picked up on the first ring, answering in a sing-songy “Annie Hutchinson, writer par excellence, at your service.”

“Very snappy,” I said, introducing myself.

“Oh yes, my father warned me that you would be calling,” she said in a tone far less welcoming than her opening line. “Based on what he said, I really don’t think I can be of any help to you.”

“Nonetheless, Miss Hutchinson, I would like to take a few minutes of your time.”

“For your information, Mr. Goodwin, I am terribly busy.”

“Too busy for lunch?”

“In this business, at least in my department, lunch is a foreign concept. You’ve probably heard that old newspaper term ‘a deadline every minute.’”

“I have.”

“Well, it’s the same here. The closest we get to a lunch break in this department is to send one of the mailroom kids down to the Automat to bring back ham sandwiches or something equally unappetizing. It's the account guys who enjoy those three-martini expense-account lunches you hear so much about."

"Life should be treating you better," I told her.

"From your lips to God's ears. If you have a question or two about my youngest sister, whom I hardly know, fire away. I have two minutes, no more."

"Sorry, Miss Hutchinson, but I prefer face-to-face conversations. How about a drink after work?"

That led to a pause at the other end. "All right, why not? I know enough about your boss to realize that you are legit, or at least as legit as a private eye can be. That's what you're called, right, a private eye?"

"In some circles, yes. Name the joint, and I will buy."

"Right on one count, wrong on the other," Annie Hutchinson said. "The joint, as you call it—I assume that's private-eye lingo—is Gerald's Public House, on Second Avenue near Fifty-Fourth, and I will buy. Six o'clock okay? That's the very earliest I can make it without getting dirty looks from a roomful of overworked colleagues."

I said six was fine, and we rang off. Next, I called Tom, the older brother, who I had learned worked as an accountant for a firm on Lexington. "Oh yeah, I've been expecting to hear from you. My father said my kid sister is in some sort of trouble and he's hired you and what's-his-name, that famous shamus?"

"Nero Wolfe. I would—"

"Before you go any further, Mr. Goodwin, I must tell you I hardly know Cordelia, even though we are currently living under the same roof over on Sutton Place. Until very recently, I was living elsewhere, and she was traveling in Europe. I really don't see how I can help you."

"I'd really like to talk to you nonetheless," I said. "How about lunch today, on me?"

He laughed. "You just hit my weak spot, Mr. Goodwin. I never say no to a free lunch. You have any place in mind?"

"I thought I would leave that to you. I am as flexible as a circus contortionist."

Another laugh. "Since you asked, I'm rather fond of La Belle Touraine, on East Fifty-First. I must warn you that it's somewhat pricey."

"Sounds good to me. I will make a reservation for noon, okay?"

"Absolutely. I'll be the tall guy with horn-rimmed glasses and a buzz haircut."

I had not been to La Belle Touraine, although I certainly knew its reputation as one of the most highly rated dining spots in town, at least in the eyes of the newspapers' food critics. After telling Fritz I would not be home for lunch, I hoofed it north to Fifty-First. Like so many New York restaurants, this one didn't look like all that much from the outside, but I had learned long ago not to judge a book by its cover, so to speak.

Inside, the set-up was like many in Midtown: a long and narrow dining room, three steps down from the entrance area, which had a small bar with a half dozen stools, all occupied. Just after I gave the tuxedoed maître d' at the podium my name and reminded him of my earlier call, a tall specimen with horn-rimmed glasses and a blondish buzz cut walked in, looking around and grinning at no one in particular. I introduced myself and we shook hands.

"Nice to meet you, Mr. Goodwin," he said, still grinning. "You can just tell by the aromas that this is one fine place, can't you?"

I agreed as we were shown to a table well toward the back, as I had specified when I made the booking. Hutchinson looked around and nodded his approval. "Yes, sir, I do love this restaurant, Mr. Goodwin."

"Glad to hear it. But please call me Archie."

"Fair enough, if you call me Tom. Now, as I said on the phone, I really don't think I can be of much help to you, Archie, although I must say that I'm curious as to just what's going on with Cordelia."

"First, how about a cocktail?"

"I shouldn't during lunch, but what the hell, it's not every day I break bread here. I'll have a vodka martini." I made an exception to my rule of avoiding alcohol at lunch and ordered a scotch and water to be sociable.

After the drinks were delivered and we had studied our menus, Tom Hutchinson leaned toward me and lowered his voice. "Cordelia isn't pregnant, is she?"

"Not as far as I know," I told him truthfully.

"I'm glad to hear that, although I would have been damned surprised to learn she was."

"Why do you say that?"

"Again, I will preface this by repeating that even though she's my sister, I really don't know her that well," Tom said after we had ordered our food. "Bear in mind that she's—what?—fourteen or fifteen years younger than I am. What I do know of her, and these last few weeks under the same roof have reinforced it, is that she tends to act awfully, well, I guess prudish, although there may be a better word to describe her. I'm not a words guy, I'm a numbers guy, so I don't have a big vocabulary."

"Like you, I don't know Cordelia very well," I said, "but having met her, I see where she certainly comes off as being somewhat prissy."

"Prissy, yeah, that's a good word. So, if she's not pregnant, what's the problem, and what do you think that I can tell you?"

he asked amiably. "I'm hardly an expert on women. You probably know at least something about my own track record."

"I know you are divorced, that's about all."

"I'll say I'm divorced, Archie, and it was ugly, damned ugly," he said, finishing his drink. "She claimed I was cheating on her, which wasn't true, not one single word of it. She was the one playing around, and it was with a so-and-so who I thought was an old friend of mine from all the way back in college. Anyway, she got a girlfriend of hers to claim I had been messing around with her. I will not bore you with all the grim details, except to say that she got her divorce, and I am well rid of the woman. Unfortunately, I'm also rid of a large chunk of my inheritance, which she got in the settlement. I may be a Hutchinson, but I am by no means a rich one, and at least for now, I'm actually back living with my parents. The one piece of good news about our split is that we had no children. Anyway, back to Cordelia. You're paying for my lunch, and you ought to get something for it."

"Cordelia is being blackmailed, and it apparently has something to do with a trip she took to Italy. Do you know anything about that?"

"I really don't, Archie. She was away about the same time that I was going through the final nasty stages of the divorce. I do know that beginning a couple of weeks ago, she has seemed very preoccupied."

"I understand she's got a serious boyfriend."

"Lance Mercer? Yes, I suppose you can say they're serious, although as far as I can tell, they haven't been seeing that much of each other lately, for whatever reason. I've only met him once. I try not to hang around the folks' place—it's embarrassing enough to live there, if only temporarily—and from what I've seen, he seems to be a lot like Cordelia. What was that word you used—*prissy*?"

"I don't generally hear it applied to a man," I said.

"Well, that's probably not the right word, then. Maybe *stiff* is better. But my parents both seem to like him; he comes from what they say is 'good stock.' And heaven knows the kid is rich, or will be. Between them, he and Cordelia should never have any money problems, don't you think?"

This time it was I who laughed. "No, it sounds like they'll be all right."

"This sole meunière is terrific," Tom said. "I had it here once before, and it's just as good this time. I hope your fish is top-drawer, too."

"It's fine, just fine." I was having the parmesan-crusted broiled scallops, and they were almost as good as Fritz's, which is saying something.

"I'd like to ask you a question, Archie."

"Shoot."

"Like I told you before, I don't hang around the Sutton Place quarters all that much, by design, but I've heard just enough at the old homestead to wonder if that shooting in Central Park the other night was somehow tied to this blackmail business you're talking about."

"I'm interested in what you have heard."

"Overheard is more like it, and before you ask, I am definitely not a snoop hanging around keyholes and half-open doors."

I laughed again. I was getting to like the guy. "So noted," I said. "Go on, I'm all ears."

"I feel like I'm some sort of traitor to the family, in a way, by talking like this, Archie. Here's what happened: I was parked in the library at home reading the evening paper one night this week, and I heard Cordelia sobbing to our father in the next room, which is his study, even though the door was shut. I gathered from those parts of the conversation I could hear that he was urging her to tell him what had been bothering her. From the fragments I picked up, she didn't sound terribly coherent, but one thing I did hear was your first name."

"Don't get any ideas, Tom. I have no romantic interest in your youngest sister, attractive as she is."

"Oh, no, no," he said, putting up a hand. "What she said seemed to do with your having been shot, silly as that sounds."

"You probably heard it wrong," I told him.

"Oh. I suppose I did. I was only getting every other word or so, and part of me was trying to listen and part of me wasn't, if you know what I mean."

"I do. Can you think of anything else that might help Mr. Wolfe and me regarding this blackmail business?"

"Not really. I just can't imagine Cordelia doing anything that would open her up to something like that. If I were to guess, I would say that she's still a virgin."

"Being a virgin doesn't necessarily protect her from a blackmailer," I said. "Especially if that blackmailer is threatening to spread lies about her."

Tom nodded thoughtfully. "I think I see where you're going, Archie. The blackmailer, whoever he is, would find some way of smearing Cordelia's name to Lance Mercer unless . . ."

"Unless?"

"Unless she coughed up some dough. And as you may already know, Cordelia is surely the richest of all of us siblings. You already know where a lot of my money flew off to, and as you might be aware, my younger brother, Doug, has frittered away his estate as well—on some sort of half-baked business venture cooked up by a none-too-bright college classmate. There's one thing Doug and I have in common: an old college 'friend' who turns out to be no friend at all. At least I've got a job, although it doesn't compensate for what I lost in the divorce settlement. All

Doug has to support himself nowadays is his artwork, which I have been told by artistic types is mediocre at best and a throwback to an earlier style."

"Not a pretty picture, no pun intended," I said.

"My sister Kathleen, who also went through a not-very-pleasant divorce recently, ended up on the short end of a settlement with her louse of a bond-trader husband, who, it turns out, wasn't very good at his job. We Hutchinsons don't tend to do very well either with marriage or with holding on to our money, do we? Have you talked to Kathleen yet?" Tom asked.

"No, although she's on my list."

"I think you will find her a very embittered woman. She has custody of the two kids—darned nice kids by the way, two little girls—and she's still holding on to her beautiful picture-book house up in Connecticut, but some day she may have to give that up and move into something smaller, although I hope not."

"Are you fond of your sister?"

"Very much," he said. "In fact, I like all my sisters a great deal. Annie is more cynical than Kathleen—see, I do know a few big words—but at heart she's a really nice person, and underneath that tough pose, very sensitive. I just wish she would find herself a man who deserves her. I hope you get a chance to meet her."

"As a matter of fact," I said as we rose to leave the restaurant, "we are having drinks tonight."

"You'll find her a most interesting person. Thanks a lot for lunch, Archie," Tom Hutchinson said as he pumped my hand on the bustling sidewalk outside La Belle Touraine. "I'm afraid I have not been all that much help to you, or to my kid sister, for that matter. I just hope that whatever kind of jam Cordelia is in, you and your boss can find a way to get her out of it."

I promised him we would give it our best efforts and headed back to the brownstone.

CHAPTER 18

Back home, I told Fritz that on top of missing lunch, I would not be around for dinner either. He gave me one of those looks that made it clear he was disappointed in me for skipping two of his meals in a row.

"Duty calls," I told him, "and believe me, I would much rather be here tonight savoring your wonderful planked porterhouse steak instead of where I will be. Can you try to save me some?"

That mollified Fritz, who allowed himself a smile. "I am glad you are working, Archie," he said, "but please do not strain yourself. You are not totally healed. I can tell by the way you carry yourself sometimes."

He was right. The shoulder bothered me when I let myself think about it. I was bandaged up tightly, and I did tend to favor the shoulder, holding my arm close to my side. Tom Hutchinson hadn't seemed to notice, but then, he had never seen me before, and maybe he figured I always walked that way.

I dropped by the office, where Wolfe was working on his post-lunch beers and perusing an orchid catalogue that had arrived in the morning mail. I gave him a brief rundown on my session with the elder Hutchinson brother, but what I related was not anywhere near as interesting as the catalogue, apparently, so I spent a few minutes tidying up my desk, which didn't need much tidying, and then I rose, stretched, yawned loudly, and said I was stepping outside to sweep off the sidewalk in front of the brownstone. When that got no reaction from the man whose nose was buried in pages with color pictures of *Cattleya*, *Brassavola*, *Miltonia*, *Odontoglossum*, and who knows what other species, I walked out of the office whistling "The Yankee Doodle Boy." Wolfe hates it when I whistle.

I climbed the stairs to my room, where I did a little more tidying up, but similar to the case with my desk, very little neatening was necessary. I then parked in my favorite chair to read a chapter or two from a biography of Winston Churchill that Wolfe had given me for my birthday. The man's speeches and his broadcasts to the English people in the roughest days of the war were impressive, no doubt about it, but for me, a little history goes a long way, so after an hour I had read enough of Dunkirk and the Blitz and the brave Spitfire pilots of the RAF and decided I needed some exercise.

I left the brownstone without a word to Wolfe, setting out to experience a sunny, balmy afternoon on the streets of Manhattan. As I walked east and then south, with no particular destination in mind, I realized I was constantly looking back to see if I was being followed. A psychologist would no doubt tell me this was angst because I had been shot at not long ago on a walk through Midtown.

Whatever the reason, I was definitely on my guard more than ever, and I wished I were as good at spotting a tail as I was at doing the tailing. I finally stopped obsessing and decided to enjoy myself. I bought a strawberry ice cream cone from a sidewalk vendor on Second Avenue, then smiled at a stunning redhead who grinned back, showing her dimples as she exited an office building at First Avenue and Forty-Fourth. A dapper mustached man who might well have served in World War One tipped his Panama hat to me and twirled his cane as he walked his schnauzer near the still-under-construction United Nations Building, which had all the architectural style of a cardboard box laid on end.

I inhaled air that seemed remarkably fresh for Manhattan and spent the rest of the afternoon wandering the city like a tourist. I felt so good that I forgot to see if anyone was following me, and the pain in my shoulder dissipated. I can't explain my carefree mood, and I probably went longer than I had in years without so much as a glance at my wristwatch. When I finally did learn the time—from a clock above the entrance to an insurance company building—I realized I had only fifteen minutes to get to Gerald's Public House for my meeting with Annie Hutchinson. Walking fast, I made it with a full two minutes to spare.

From the street, Gerald's presented itself as an English or Irish pub, with its frosted, multi-paned windows and a painted wooden sign hanging out over the sidewalk that proclaimed "Lagers, Ales, and Stouts from the World Over." I walked in, expecting a deafening blast of jukebox music, and was pleasantly surprised to hear a muted version of Gershwin's "Rhapsody in Blue" being piped in through some sort of sound system.

A long bar spanned one wall on the left side of the narrow room, with padded booths strung out along the opposite wall. The place was less than half full. I looked around, realizing I never asked Annie Hutchinson how I would recognize her. I needn't have worried.

"I suspect you of being Archie Goodwin," a soft but firm voice from behind me intoned. I turned to see that the voice belonged to a sandy-haired, oval-faced, blue-eyed woman of small-to-medium height whose beige dress subtly hinted at her curves. Her smile, while less than welcoming, was far from hostile. I liked her overall appearance.

"Guilty as charged, your honor," I said. "Do I look like an Archie Goodwin?"

She cocked her head, hands on hips. "Well, you are too well dressed to fit my preconception of a private detective," she said. "But, one, you also are someone I have never seen in here before; two, it is six o'clock; and three, you look like you are waiting for someone. Is that what is called 'deductive reasoning' in your business?"

I grinned down at her. "I will give you a passing grade in Detection 101. What is your pleasure, bar stool or booth?"

"Remember, this is on me, so that is the question that I should be asking you."

"Okay, then I will cast my vote for a booth. That way, we can face each other."

"Face each other, eh? You make it sound like an interrogation. Do you, Mr. Archie Goodwin, plan to interrogate me?"

"Heaven forbid," I told her as we slid into one of the booths. "I prefer to call what we are about to have a conversation."

"Fine by me, sounds very civilized," Annie replied as a waiter came over. "What will you have?"

I looked at her, and she said, "You first. You're the guest."

"Scotch and water."

"Any particular brand, sir?"

"No, so long as it wasn't distilled in the basement here."

The young man, probably either a college student or an aspiring actor—or maybe both—gave me a quizzical look and turned to Annie.

"An old-fashioned," she said.

After he left, she frowned at me. "You were not very nice to him. He's just a kid trying to make his way."

"Hey, I was just giving you a little taste of private-eye humor."

"Very little and not very humorous," she parried, suppressing a laugh.

I shook a finger at her and grinned. "Hah, caught you about to giggle."

"Enough of this silliness," she said. "You suggested this meeting to discuss what I know about the woman I think of as my baby sister. Let's get on with it."

"You are all business; I like that," I replied as the drinks were set in front of us. I smiled at our waiter to show that I was really a nice person, down deep. He walked away, and I turned back to Annie. "Your baby sister, as you call her, is being blackmailed."

"Cordelia, really? Whatever for?" Annie seemed genuinely surprised.

"Your father didn't tell you?"

"No. He phoned me and said you would be calling each of us—me, my other sister, and my brothers. All I was told was that Cordelia was in some kind of trouble and that he had hired Nero Wolfe to investigate. Wolfe I have heard of, you I have not. I mean no offense by that."

"None taken. I'm just a lackey."

"Are you now?" she said, arching an eyebrow and taking a sip of her drink. "I find that hard to believe. You certainly do not seem like someone who I would term a lackey."

"Believe what you will. Something apparently happened to Cordelia on her trip to Italy earlier this year, and she is terrified it will come to light if she doesn't pay someone off—someone whose identity she is not even aware of."

"Are you telling me that you don't know what transpired over there?"

"Your younger sister is being very circumspect."

"Cordelia . . . circumspect? She wouldn't know the meaning of the word. You have met her, haven't you?"

"Yes."

"Then you have to know that the girl is incapable of subtlety of any kind. As I'm sure you are aware, she came along years later than the rest of us, and she is a perfect example of what I call the 'Surprise Child Syndrome.'"

"Meaning what?"

She pulled out a cigarette and fired it up before I could reach my lighter. "Meaning she was spoiled, doted on, from day one. Our parents treated her like some sort of porcelain doll that had to be protected from all manner of dangers out in the big, bad world. It is hardly surprising that she's turned out to be so damned ingenuous, all wide-eyed and gullible."

"Do you think at least some of that behavior is an act on her part?"

"Not a chance. She's simply not clever enough to be able to pull something like that off."

"You don't seem fond of Cordelia, to say the least."

"Oh, I'm sorry to sound so bitchy, pay me no mind," she said, waving a manicured hand dismissively. "It's really not her fault that she's turned out the way she has. Do you have even a clue about this so-called blackmailing business? After all, you're supposed to be a detective."

"I have a feeling it somehow has to do with a man."

"Doesn't everything?" Annie said, bitterness creeping into her voice. "Men are the source of all evil, and I don't know you well enough to let you off the hook and say 'present company excepted.'"

"I'll see if I can behave in such a way as to free myself from your blanket indictment. Tell me about Cordelia's love life."

"Such as it is. You must know that she has been spending a lot of time with that Mercer boy."

"I'm aware of that. What do you think of him?"

She shrugged. "I've only met him, what, twice, no, three times. He seems as bland as Cordelia, so I suppose they're suited for each other. My parents are all for it. For one thing, they like the idea that Lance Mercer can't possibly be marrying her for her money because he's got piles of it himself, or will have some day."

"I hear that she has put their engagement on hold, though," I said.

"Really? Then you know more than I do, Mr. Goodwin, which isn't surprising, given how rarely I drop by the posh family abode."

"Call me Archie, please. Are you and your parents at odds?"

"Not exactly . . . Archie. But whenever I do show up at the Sutton Place palace, as I call it, they start grilling me about my social life, who am I seeing, when am I going to settle down, and on and on."

"What do you tell them?"

Annie grinned. "To mind their own business. Not that directly, of course. I really do love them both, but I make it clear that I'm going to live my own life without anyone telling me how it should be done—or with whom."

"Seems a reasonable response," I said. "Way back when I left Ohio to come here, I essentially told my folks the same thing."

"How did they take it?"

"Not well at first, but there wasn't a lot they could do to stop me. To please them, I had given college a stab, but it wasn't to my liking, and I left almost as soon as I had begun. My father is long dead, but my mother and I are on good terms."

"As long as we're asking each other personal questions, I'll try another one: Are you married?"

"No, although I have a very good friend, and my mother, who comes here once a year for a week or so, seems comfortable with that. She has met the lady in question and likes her."

"Well, that's good to hear," Annie said. "I want to get back to Cordelia, since that's the reason we are here. Sometimes I am a little slow, but I am just now beginning to put two and two together. She was in Italy, and she is being blackmailed. *Why?* I ask myself. Because of a man, of course, you suggested as much yourself.

"Now, I have spent some time in Italy myself, and I know more than a little about the habits of Italian men, particularly as those habits relate to female tourists. Are you following me?"

"I'm hanging on your every word."

"How nice. Anyway, I will lay odds that all of this has to do with some Italian of the male species. When I first heard that Cordelia was going to Italy alone, it occurred to me that, given her innocence, it was like leading a lamb to the slaughter."

"Interesting theory," I said. "Let us assume you are right. If so, who might the blackmailer be?"

"I have no idea whatsoever. Maybe it's someone in Italy, threatening her long distance. As you probably know, Cordelia is rich, very rich. Our parents have been extremely good to her."

"And to you all as well, I am sure."

"Yes, but as the favorite child—and make no mistake, that's what she is—Cordelia has always been given special treatment."

"Do I detect a hint of jealousy?"

Annie gave me a tight smile. "Maybe just a hint. Since the day I left college, I have always held a job and worked hard. I don't know the details of how evenly our parents have spread their money around to us and I haven't asked, but I do know that my father tends to play favorites."

"Meaning Cordelia is one of them?"

"Yes, maybe the only one. My brother Doug, for instance, made an unwise investment that apparently ate up most, if not all, of his inheritance, and my father has in effect said to him 'no more from me.' Have you talked to Doug?"

"No, so far just Tom."

"Ah yes. Then as you probably know, he lost a large portion of his share to that harpy he was married to. My parents are not the least bit sympathetic to his current plight, as they never liked the woman and strongly advised him against marrying her. They could easily have settled more money on Tom, as they could have on Doug, but they chose not to."

"That leaves your other sister."

"Poor Kathleen. So far, this generation of the Hutchinson clan has not done well in the matrimony department. It is no wonder I've stayed single. Kathleen married a Wall Street bond trader, damned handsome fellow named Lawrence who seemed to have everything going for him: old-line Boston family, Ivy League degree, job with a gold-plated firm."

"Sounds good so far," I said.

"Doesn't it? But this character turned out to be all façade and no substance. And very little in the way of responsibility. First off, his 'old-line' Boston roots were rotten. His family, who once had a townhouse on Louisburg Square, which is the Sutton Place of Boston, had lost almost everything during the Depression, although he hid that fact from my parents, who thought it was wonderful that their daughter was marrying into New England society. Then we learned he had gotten into college on a need-based scholarship and just barely had the grades to graduate."

"Now the story doesn't sound nearly as good."

"Wait, Archie, sadly there's more to come. It turned out that Lawrence wasn't very skilled at trading bonds and got fired by that well-known Wall Street firm. Then, living on her money while he presumably was looking for another job, he started drinking and playing around. Kathleen finally divorced him—they had two children by this time—and she was so glad to be rid of him that she gave him all the money he asked for, which apparently was plenty.

"My father was furious with her for caving in so easily and told her she wasn't getting any more money from him."

"So, how is she surviving now?"

"Well, she's not broke, if that's what you mean. She still has the fine house up in Connecticut that she essentially paid for herself. And she still has enough to get by on, but I gather from what she has said to me that things are pretty tight. I didn't mean to go on so about the trials and tribulations of the younger Hutchinsons. I feel like a society-page gossip columnist."

"You have been very helpful," I said. "Now comes the hardest question of all: Do you think any one of your siblings is behind the blackmailing?"

Annie jerked upright. "I certainly do not, Archie. That suggestion is simply ludicrous!"

"But is it? It sounds like several of your siblings are in financial straits of varying degrees, while Cordelia certainly is not. It is by no means unheard-of for one family member to blackmail another, and usually for financial reasons. I can remember a case—"

"I still say that it's preposterous. Like me, none of them is without sin, but I simply refuse to believe any one of them would do such a thing."

"All right. Do you happen to know a woman named Marlene Peters?" I asked.

"No, should I?"

"Not necessarily."

"Now it is my turn to ask a question," Annie said. "First, I am sure you have heard of Allard & Brooks Advertising."

"I don't think I have—why?"

"Are you being petulant now?"

"What on earth would I have to be petulant about?"

"You are upset because I did not know who *you* were, but I *did* know about your boss."

"I told you there was no offense taken about that."

"So you say. But consider that A&B is far and away the best-known shop in New York, if not the whole country. And you telephoned me there, so you had to know about the place."

"I'm not going to get into an argument with you over this," I told her, "but the only thing I knew about you was that you worked for an advertising agency, and not its name. Your father gave me a phone number where you could be reached, nothing more. I know very little about the world of advertising."

"All right," Annie said. "I apologize, especially since I am about to ask a favor of you."

"Apology accepted," I said as a second round of drinks arrived. "As for the favor, I withhold judgment for the present."

"Hear me out, Archie," she said. "A&B has just won our biggest account of the year, Remmers Beer, which we took away from its long-time agency. I believe you have heard of the brand."

"I have," I replied with a grin. "Go on."

"Your boss drinks Remmers, of course, and has for years. I know that because the brewery has in its files a newspaper profile of Nero Wolfe from some years back that mentions his preference for Remmers."

"I recall the article. My boss was never interviewed for the piece, but a former client of ours told the reporter about Mr. Wolfe's liking for that particular brand, among other things. That man will never be a client again."

"So that's how it is," she said.

"That's precisely how it is. Mr. Wolfe values his privacy."

Annie took a pen and a sheet of paper from her purse and scribbled something on the sheet, sliding it across the table to me. "How much would he value that?"

She had printed numbers on the sheet, a dollar sign followed by a figure that had several zeros. "What's the play?" I asked.

"The play, Archie, is this: We at A&B want Nero Wolfe to be the prime endorser of Remmers. Color magazine photos of him at his desk with a bottle; TV and radio spots; the works. Even billboards along all the major roads leading into the city."

"Now it is my turn to use the word *preposterous*, Annie—that is, if I may call you Annie?"

She nodded.

"Nero Wolfe will never, I repeat *never*, sit still for something like this. He would rather take a cab ride to Newark, and he detests taxis and all other wheeled vehicles, with the possible exception of his own automobile with me at the wheel, and then only on special occasions."

"But the money . . ."

"Forget the money. He likes the green stuff, yes, as we all do. But sometimes, the cost of obtaining it is simply too great. That would be the case here."

"But from his standpoint, wouldn't it be good for business?"

"Maybe marginally, but bear in mind that Nero Wolfe has never advertised, not once. Yet word-of-mouth has kept him busy for years. And there's one more thing, Annie. I understand you and the others in your agency are experts on what sells a product, but do you really think that you want a spokesman for your beer who weighs a seventh of a ton?"

That stopped her cold. She looked at me, and then down at her half-empty glass and back at me again. "For some reason, I think I like you. Care to stay right where we are and have dinner?"

"You've got yourself a deal," I told her.

"But only on the condition that I also pay for the meal," Annie said, holding up a hand. "You may not like the food, so you shouldn't have to foot the bill for it."

"I'll take my chances," I told her.

"The pub grub in here is pretty darn good, I can attest to that," Annie said as we were handed menus. "Of course, I know from that newspaper article I read about Nero Wolfe that he has a live-in chef who prepares world-class meals for him. Do you get to eat those meals as well?"

I said I did, but assured her that I was by no means a food snob. I had fish and chips while she went with the shepherd's pie. "This is all right stuff," I told her. "Do you eat here often?"

"Maybe once a week. It's less than two blocks from the agency. I'm not a bad cook, if I do say so myself, so most nights I whip up something for dinner at my place over in Brooklyn Heights. My specialty is beef bourguignon, but I also make a damned fine chicken cacciatore."

"Mark me down as impressed," I told her as we continued to tackle our meals. I knew she was leading up to an invitation to her place, and I wanted to head that off. I asked a few more questions about Cordelia and her other siblings, but nothing of interest surfaced. The longer we talked, the more it became clear that Annie really didn't see other members of her family very often, apparently by choice. We finished our dinner and lingered over a cup of coffee.

"Please let me hail a cab for you," I said as we were leaving the pub. "That is the very least I can do, given that you popped for both drinks and dinner, for which I give my thanks."

"It was my pleasure," Annie said, "even though you shot down my idea about having your boss be a spokesman for Remmers."

"If it makes you feel better, I will pass the offer along to him, if only to get his reaction."

"Why not? Maybe he will surprise you."

I had no trouble flagging down a taxi. Opening the door for Annie, I leaned over to say goodnight.

"Keep in touch, Archie," she said, smiling up at me as she slipped in. "I want to know how this business with Cordelia turns out. And despite what I said about her, I really do love my baby sister. I know that I tend to be sarcastic and caustic sometimes, but for what it's worth, I'm trying to overcome that tendency."

CHAPTER 19

After Annie's cab pulled away, I grabbed a taxi of my own and went straight to the brownstone. I bypassed the office and went to the kitchen, where Fritz was puttering around. "Save me any of that planked porterhouse?"

He shook his head. "I am sorry, Archie, but Mr. Wolfe invited a guest for dinner, so there is none left."

"A guest, eh? Who was it?"

"Mr. Panzer."

"Interesting. Did he stay long?"

"They talked for quite a while in the office after they finished eating," Fritz said.

I wasn't sure what Wolfe was up to, but more than once over the years, he has given Saul assignments without telling me about them. When I complained, I was told, "I don't want to distract you from what you are currently working on. I have another assignment for Saul."

I was damned if I was going to ask Wolfe why he needed Saul this time, so instead of going into the office, I went upstairs to my room. He would get my reports on Tom and Annie Hutchinson when I was ready to give them, not before.

The next morning, after finishing breakfast, I put in a call to Doug, the Greenwich Village member of the Hutchinson family. He answered on the sixth or seventh ring, his voice fuzzy. I introduced myself, although my name didn't seem to register with him.

"I think your father told you I would be calling," I said.

"Uh . . . maybe so. I . . . Can I call you back?"

"If you are free today, how about lunch? Name the place. I'll buy."

"Tell me what this is about . . . I forget." His voice was slightly clearer now.

"Your sister Cordelia is having some problems, and your father has hired Nero Wolfe, the private investigator, to help her. Mr. Wolfe is my boss."

"Oh . . . okay, yeah, I think I remember. Who are you again?"

I told him, spelling my last name. I felt like I was having a conversation with a fifth-grader who was not near the top of his class.

"Uh, lunch, right? What . . . what do you want to know?"

"Let's discuss that when we are together. I can meet you whenever and wherever you say."

"Um, let's see, it's now . . . What time have you got?"

"Nine-twenty."

A muffled groan came through the wire. "What about, oh . . . one o'clock?"

"One is just fine with me, Mr. Hutchinson. Where would you like to eat? Make it easy on yourself."

"You, um, you know where the Village is?"

I told him I did.

"Okay, yeah, well, there's this deli on Bleecker, a couple of doors down from Christopher," he said between yawns. "This place, it doesn't have a name that I know of, just a red wooden sign over the door that says 'Deli.'"

"A deli called 'Deli,' huh? Okay, I'll meet you out in front at one. How will I recognize you?"

"Big sunglasses," he muttered. "Yeah, big sunglasses."

I rang off and hoped that within the next three-plus hours, Doug Hutchinson would manage to pull himself together and become more alert than he had been on the telephone. Last night must have been a doozy—unless, of course, he awoke in a similar state every morning.

I took a taxi downtown and jumped off a block from the intersection of Bleecker and Christopher. The weather was as nice as it had been the day before, and the neighborhood was crowded with pedestrians, as is usually the case in the Village, good weather or bad. I spotted the deli with its big red sign before I had gotten within a half block. I parked myself outside the front door and waited. And waited.

At one fifteen, a short, slim, sandy-haired man of indeterminate age wearing oversized sunglasses walked up to me. "Would you be Mr. Goodwin?" His voice possessed more strength than earlier in the day.

"That's me. And I take it you are Doug Hutchinson."

"You take it right," he said. "How ya doin'?"

"Just fine. By the way, you didn't sound so good on the phone earlier. Are you okay?" I asked as we entered the deli.

That brought a chuckle. "Yeah, I had sort of a late night. There was an opening at one of the galleries near here, and the party went on longer than any of us figured it would."

"That's right, you're an artist," I said as we eased into a booth toward the rear of the noisy joint. "What do you specialize in?"

"Are you an art lover?" he asked.

"Not in a sophisticated sense. I'm just one of those who knows what he likes when he sees it."

Another chuckle. "Most people are that way, which is fine, I don't knock it," Doug said as we each ordered a corned beef sandwich on rye from a waitress who looked to be about fifteen but was probably older. "There are too damn many snobs in the art world. Me, I'm kind of a throwback, you might say. Do you happen to know what cubism is?"

"I would be lying if I said I did, although I have heard the term."

He nodded. "It was a popular movement and a damned important one early in the century. Picasso was a big part of it, along with Braque, Léger, Gris, and a few others. I decided to become a cubist, or really a neo-cubist, which makes me out of step with the times. But I like the style and always have. And if I do say so myself, I've gotten some good reviews in the local papers for my oils and charcoals. One critic even called me 'a worthy successor to Georges Braque.'"

"That had to make you feel good."

"It did, but not as good as when I actually met Braque in Paris a few years back and showed him photos of some of my work. He clapped me on the back, grinned, and gave me a thumbs-up sign."

"Do your paintings sell?" I asked.

He shook his head. "I figured that question was coming sooner or later. No, I haven't done all that well, although there are a handful of collectors—a very small handful—who like cubism but can't find the early works on the market, so they settle for me and my much cheaper prices."

"Interesting. But I'm really here to talk about your youngest sister and her problems."

Doug took off his sunglasses, exposing tired red eyes. "My

dear old father, who I almost never hear from anymore, phoned and told me Cordelia was in some sort of trouble, and that you would be calling me. That's all he said—he didn't go into any detail—so I have no idea what is going on or how I can be of any help."

"I'm not sure you can help, but I do appreciate your taking the time to talk to me. Cordelia's problems appear to stem from a trip she took to Italy."

"Oh yeah, her famous Italian adventure. So, did she get into some trouble over there?"

"She is apparently being blackmailed."

He frowned. "What on earth for? I assume you've met her. She's as innocent as a newborn babe. What kind of trouble could she possibly get into?"

"She is being very close-mouthed about the whole business, won't even give her parents any details. Nero Wolfe and I thought maybe she had confided in one or more of her siblings."

"Have you talked to any of them yet?" Doug asked between bites of his sandwich.

"Yes, both Tom and Annie, and neither of them has any clue as to what the problem is."

"I'm not surprised. Cordelia's almost half a generation younger than the rest of us. I am the next youngest, and I'm ten years older than she is—almost eleven, really. I never had all that much to do with her growing up. Hell, I was already out of college—for all the good that did me—just about the time that she was entering high school."

"I understand that when Cordelia was in Italy, she met up with a friend of hers, Marlene Peters."

He frowned, as if thinking. "Oh . . . I guess maybe I had heard something about that."

"I also understand you have gone out with Miss Peters."

"Oh, that!" he said, waving it away with a hand. "For some reason, Cordelia thought we might hit it off, even though I'm a good ten years older than Marlene, too. She's a nice girl, a lot of fun. And yeah, we did go out a few times, but it just didn't click, if you know what I mean?"

"Yes, I've been there myself, more than once. Do you have any idea where Marlene Peters lives?"

"Last I knew, she was somewhere over east of the Village, close to the river, but it's been a while."

"Do you have any other thoughts about Cordelia? Is she harboring any deep, dark secrets you're aware of?"

Doug laughed so loudly that people in nearby booths turned toward us. "Does Miss Oh-So-Proper have any secrets? I couldn't even begin to guess what they are," he said. "She really doesn't seem like the type. She does have a boyfriend, though—do you know about that?"

"A little. Lance Mercer, right?"

"That's the one. I've never met him, but I do know that he comes from money, lots of it, airplanes. In that respect, he and Cordelia have something in common. They'll never have to worry about paying the bills."

"She's got a large inheritance, doesn't she?"

"Damn right she does. I did once, too. Maybe you know about that," Doug said, his tone suddenly defensive.

"Not much," I told him. "My main focus in this investigation is your youngest sister."

"Well, as long as you're here and you took the time to grill me, I'll spell it out. What the hell, who cares? I've never been what you would call a favorite of my parents, particularly my father. My older brother, whom you've met, decided early on that he wanted to go into accounting, a duller choice I can't begin to imagine. Anyway, that left me as the last hope in the family to follow the old man into the railroad business. The idea of me going into railroading is about as absurd as Harry Truman becoming a touring golf pro. Even though I loved art as a kid and majored in it in college, my father still thought I might have a change of heart and go to work playing with trains, and not the type that run around a Christmas tree.

"I made it clear that world wasn't for me, which was strike one, as far as Dear Old Dad was concerned. Then I moved into a loft down in this neighborhood. That made me a 'beatnik,' which ranks somewhere down there with 'communist' as far as he is concerned. Strike two. And then I invested big bucks in a trading company with a friend from college. It collapsed like a house of cards, and there went my inheritance, *poof!* I never knew that so much money could disappear so fast. Strike three. In just a few sentences, that's my story. Do you think it would make a novel?"

"I'm afraid you are asking the wrong guy," I told him, trying to lighten the mood. "I know as much about literature as you say you know about railroading."

"Touché!" Doug said, clapping his hands. "I realize that I haven't been much help to you," he went on. "Sorry, but what you see before you is the black sheep of the family, an outcast. Sort of like a leper, you know?"

I could see that Doug Hutchinson was beginning to wallow in self-pity, which is never a pretty sight. It usually manifests when someone has had too much to drink, but his only beverage at lunch was coffee, and not a lot of that. I thanked him for his time and rose, leaving a tip on the table.

"Thanks for lunch," he said, waving a hand and staying seated. "'Preciate it."

CHAPTER 20

That left one more Hutchinson offspring to meet: the divorced Kathleen Willis up in New England, plus Marlene Peters, who, according to Doug, lived east of the Village. I had their telephone numbers, and it would have been far easier to try Miss Peters first, in the hopes I might find her at home or at her place of work—either of the locations being far closer to my present location than Westport, Connecticut.

But it was a beautiful day, and I was in the mood to commune with nature. End of internal discussion. I found a phone booth along Bleecker, pumped the necessary coins into it, got Kathleen right away, and identified myself.

"Oh yes, Daddy told me I would be hearing from you," she said in a tone somewhere between indifferent and icy. "Something to do with a problem Cordelia is having, I believe."

"Yes, and I was hoping to—"

"There is really nothing I can think of that would help with whatever happens to be going on, Mr. Goodwin. I doubt if I have seen Cordelia more than three times in the last two years or so, and then we exchanged only a few words. It's not that I don't like her—after all, she is a sister—but we have next to nothing in common, other than the same parents. When we do see each other, we have almost nothing to say except 'my, you're looking good,' or 'I just love your new hairstyle.'"

"Nevertheless, I would like to come up to Westport and talk to you. I promise not to waste your time."

"You want to come here today?" She sounded surprised, and definitely not happy.

"I vow to be brief. Scout's honor, Mrs. Willis."

That brought the hint of a chuckle. "'Scout's honor.' I haven't heard that term in years. Were you really a Boy Scout, Mr. Goodwin?"

"For a spell, yes. Then I discovered girls, and all of a sudden, Scouts didn't seem quite so much fun."

"I'll bet you are a stitch at parties with your snappy patter."

"I would be delighted to give you a chance to find out firsthand."

This time, the chuckle was full-blown and pleasant to hear. "All right, come ahead. I assume you are driving and will need some directions."

"Yes to both," I told her, and was given the directions to her place in Westport.

I like driving but don't get to do a lot of it in and around Manhattan, which is a good walking town and has armies of taxis and buses, as well as what the city claims to be the world's greatest subway system, never mind what London says. It was a pleasure to ease the roadster—Wolfe's "other" car—out of Curran's Motors.

Steering north and then east, I left New York City in my rearview mirror and passed signs announcing exits for Mount Vernon, New Rochelle, and White Plains before entering Connecticut on the tree-lined Merritt Parkway, called "the most beautiful road in America" by some. I hadn't seen enough of the country to evaluate that claim, but without question, the parkway is scenic and forested, pleasantly absent of billboards or anything that seems remotely urban.

I got off at Westport and followed Kathleen Willis's detailed directions, winding through a town that could have been designed as Hollywood's idea of an ideal New England village. The Willis house was three blocks from the small business district. Perched on a small rise above the street, the two-story red brick Georgian mansion with white shutters and columns flanking the front door seemed to be saying "approach with caution."

I parked in front and walked up the five-step stone stairway cut into the grassy rise. Before I could rap on the brass knocker, the paneled front door swung open, revealing a tall, svelte woman with long, wavy, ash-blond hair that covered one eye. Shades of Veronica Lake.

"Are you the former Boy Scout?" she asked, raising an eyebrow. I gave her the Scout salute as I remembered it.

"Nicely done, come in," she said, gracefully stepping aside. "You made good time—that is, unless you were calling me from Higgins Drug Store two minutes from here."

"No, I really did telephone from the big, bad city one state over. Your directions were so good that I made all the correct turns and hardly ever broke the speed limit. Scout's honor."

"I'm proud of you," she said, looking back over her shoulder and smiling as she led me through a chandeliered entry hall big enough to hold an eight-piece dance band. She had a good figure and knew how to show it off without flaunting it. "We can sit in the sun room and talk, if that is all right with you, Mr. Goodwin."

"It's jake with me. And I answer to Archie."

"All right, Archie," she replied, directing me to a white wicker chair that looked out on a terraced backyard where two grade-school-age girls were playing in a sandbox. "My kids, Laura and Meg," their mother said. "Can I get you something to drink, coffee perhaps, or lemonade?"

"Coffee would be fine—black."

Kathleen left and returned no more than two minutes later with two cups and a silver pot. She poured java into the cups, handed one to me, and took a chair at a right angle to mine, crossing one nylon-sheathed leg over the other. They were fine legs.

"Now, tell me just what is going on with Cordelia," she said.

"That is what we are trying to find out," I recited. "We know she's being blackmailed, but she is very close-mouthed about the reason. Your father has tried without success to get her to open up. Mr. Wolfe and I are hoping one of her siblings might have some thoughts."

"Have you talked to the others?"

I nodded. "Yes, all of them."

"Was anyone able to shed any light on the situation?"

"No, not really."

"Then I am puzzled as to why you think I can help. Of all of us, I am probably the one least close to Cordelia, not that any of our generation is what you would term really close to her. She came along much later, as I am sure you know, being a keen-eyed detective."

"Keen-eyed?" I laughed. "I would like to think so, of course. But so far, we haven't been able to figure out who might be applying the screws to your younger sister."

"Clearly someone who knows she has money," Kathleen said, shifting and tucking one leg under her. "Of all of us, she's the one who's the best off financially, and by far."

"These digs of yours certainly don't look bad," I observed, looking around.

"No, they are not bad at all, but do not let appearances fool you, Mr. Archie Goodwin. I paid dearly to hold on to this house. I made a bad marriage, as you are probably aware."

"I have heard something to that effect."

She sniffed. "I'll just bet you have, and you don't have to bother being diplomatic with me. I know very well the kinds of things being said by members of my family. When I met Lawrence Willis, I thought I had found the right person to spend my life with." Another sniff. "Was I ever wrong about *that*!"

I drank the coffee—which was quite good—and nodded. She clearly wanted to talk, and I was not about to get in her way.

"Lawrence—he never wanted to be called Larry, said that was too middle class—gave a great first impression. He was damned good-looking. Still is, although he's getting a little frayed around the edges, you might say, and a bit on the paunchy side. When we met, he had recently graduated from Brown, although I later learned he barely staggered through to get his degree. He claimed his parents came from old-line Boston money, but it turned out that money had been lost years before, in the Depression, along with the grand family home on Louisburg Square."

She paused to refill our cups. "Please don't get me wrong, Archie. I am not a fortune hunter, and I did not marry Lawrence because of any money I thought he had. I felt I had been given enough myself. But as I learned, he was the one looking for a rich spouse. His so-called "big job" on Wall Street turned out to be low-level, and he ended up losing even that. Then there was the drinking, and the . . . well, you really don't want to listen to me going on with this litany of my woes—I've bored enough others with that over the years.

"I'll just leave it that I was so anxious to get out of the marriage that I gave Lawrence everything he asked for except this house. My father thought I caved in too quickly and that I should have fought him much more vigorously, but I honestly didn't have the stomach for it."

"Where is he now?" I asked.

"In an apartment over in downtown Stamford, a very nice set-up, my daughters tell me. I have never been there. He sees them on weekends, comes here to pick them up."

"Is he employed now?"

"Yes, in a brokerage house near where he lives. I don't think he's making all that much money, but then he does not have to, given the amount that he's gotten out of me."

"Quite a story."

"Isn't it, though? Sorry to bore you."

"You haven't, not at all. Given your knowledge of Cordelia, which I can understand is limited, do you have any thoughts at all as to why someone would be blackmailing her?"

"No, none whatever. She is a somewhat naive girl, as I'm sure you have figured out, but I should think that along with naïveté would come caution."

"Good point. I understand she has a special friend."

"Yes, the Mercer boy. I can't say I know him, although I've met him once or twice. He seems very reserved, or maybe just shy. You can't think that he'd be a blackmailer, can you?"

"I haven't met him, and even if I had, I don't do the thinking in our operation. I leave that to Mr. Wolfe."

"You are very modest," Kathleen said. "I suspect you do a great deal of thinking. I'm interested in what you think about my brothers and older sister."

"They are all interesting people."

"That is a non-answer, Archie Goodwin. You must have some opinions."

"So now *you're* the one doing the questioning," I said with a grin. "All right, here's a quick rundown: I found Tom to be likable and friendly; Annie to be bright, inquisitive, and somewhat aggressive; and Doug to be on the defensive side."

"I'm not surprised at any of your observations. Of the three, I am most concerned about Doug. Tom will survive divorce and will ultimately be the better for it; Annie will move up the advertising ladder and maybe even find a man in the process; but Doug . . ."

"Go on after the *but*," I prompted.

She shifted in her chair. "Doug doesn't seem to be going anywhere. You probably know about his failed business venture. He is in much worse financial shape than me, and he and my father are barely on speaking terms. Dad advised against his getting into that deal with a college classmate, but Doug thought he knew it all, and he lost just about everything he had."

"And from what he told me, he doesn't sell much of his art."

"I've heard the same thing from him," Kathleen said. "I am not knowledgeable enough about art to be a good judge of his work, but I like it. There's an example that he gave me," she said, turning and pointing at a framed oil painting on the wall that looked like a bunch of children's blocks jumbled together, but without any letters or numbers on them. The predominant colors were brown and yellow. "That is what's called cubism," she said.

"At least I can tell how it got its name," I remarked.

She laughed. "Not everybody likes cubism, which has been around for at least half a century. Why my brother is tackling a genre that has gone out of style, I really can't say. But then, Doug always has had a contrary streak. Maybe it has to do with the so-called 'artistic temperament.'"

"What is his social life like?"

"I really don't know," Kathleen said. "He's living in his own very private world down there in the Village, and he seems to like it that way. I think he went out a few times with a friend of Cordelia's, whose name I forgot if I ever even knew it. But I gather that relationship didn't lead anywhere, maybe because he was quite a bit older than she."

"Well, I've taken enough of your time," I told her as I rose to leave. "I appreciate your having seen me on such short notice."

"I know I haven't been much help, for which I am truly sorry. I hate to see Cordelia in some sort of trouble, whatever it is. She is really a decent kid, although at her age, she's hardly a kid anymore, right? But to me she seems so much younger than she really is."

"And to me as well," I said, shaking her hand and stepping out into Connecticut's balmy summer afternoon.

CHAPTER 21

On the drive back to New York, I considered the plights of the Hutchinson siblings: two bloodied survivors of rancorous divorces; one successful but apparently dissatisfied advertising copywriter; an artist who was broke and going nowhere; and a guileless tourist who had met one charming and slick-talking Italian too many. Whoever it was that warned of "the trials of abounding wealth" certainly knew what he was talking about. Over lunch, Doug had wondered aloud about whether his misfortunes were the stuff of a novel. I wasn't sure about that, but if you took the experiences of each member of the younger Hutchinson generation and put them all together, they would make quite a saga, and not a particularly happy or uplifting one.

It was almost four thirty when I returned to the brownstone after having dropped the roadster off at the garage. Wolfe was up in the greenhouse enjoying his afternoon session with the orchids and Fritz bustled around the kitchen preparing the evening meal.

"Will you be dining with us tonight, Archie?" he asked, a touch of scolding in his tone.

"Yes, I have missed far too many of your fine meals lately, and it is time I put a stop to that. Notice that I am not even going to ask you about tonight's menu, because whatever it is will be better than anything I have had outside these walls over the last few days."

That put a smile on Fritz's puss. He would deny it if asked, but he loves to hear praise for his culinary skills—and they merit quite a bit of praise.

"Tonight, I am serving one of your favorites: veal bird in casserole with mushrooms and white wine. I do remember that the last time I served it, you talked about it for days," Fritz said.

"It was well worth talking about for days. I'm not sure how I can stand to wait until seven, but somehow I will manage."

I left Fritz a happy man and went to the office to telephone Marlene Peters, the last person on my to-be-interviewed list. Cordelia had given me two numbers for Marlene: her apartment on the Lower East Side and the bookshop in the same neighborhood where she lived. There was no answer at home, so I dialed the number at the store.

"Mason's Book Nook," a young-sounding female voice chirped.

"I would like to speak to Marlene Peters."

"This is she. How may I help you?" I told her who I was and why I was calling. There was silence for several seconds. "How did you get my number?" she demanded, no longer chirping.

I told her that Cordelia had given it to me.

"Well, I really can't imagine why," she snapped. "I was in Florence when she was, that much is true, but I certainly don't know about any sort of blackmailing. It really sounds terrible."

"Yes, it does, and Cordelia is extremely upset, as I'm sure you can imagine. My boss, Nero Wolfe, and I are trying to determine who the blackmailer is. It would be helpful if I could talk to you about your time in Florence with Cordelia. Without even realizing it, you may have some insights."

"I am sorry, Mr. . . . Goodwin. I'm at work and really am not free to talk. Even if I could, I don't know what I could say that would be of any help."

"What time do you get off today?"

"Nine o'clock, that's when we close up."

"Fine, I'll stop by then. We can get a cup of coffee or a sandwich someplace nearby. Where is the shop?"

"On Second Avenue, just north of Sixth Street. But I really don't see any use in this."

"Consider it as doing a favor for your good friend. And if you are worried about me, I can only say that I am honest and trustworthy. You can call Cordelia and ask her about me. When we meet, I will show you my private investigator's license, complete with a picture. It was issued to me by the great State of New York, and they have never had reason to revoke it."

I could hear deep breathing. "Well . . . all right, as long as Cordelia said you should call me. I'll try to remember everything I can think of about the time when she and I were together in Florence."

When Wolfe came down from the plant rooms at six, I told him where I had been and where I would be later in the evening. He held fast in his insistence that I wait until after my meeting with Marlene Peters to give him the rundown on all of my interviews. "I do not want to receive these reports in piecemeal form," he grumped. "Your memory is good enough to store everything up until such time as you can repeat it all to me."

I appreciated his faith in my ability to give verbatim reports on extended conversations, although I would have liked to unload some of my information then. But Wolfe is a genius and I am not, so that settled the matter without further discussion.

The veal bird casserole was as good as I had remembered, maybe even better, and it was followed by a dessert of raspberries in sherry cream, another of my all-time favorites. Could this be Fritz's way of reminding me just how much I had been missing recently?

Wolfe stuck to his inflexible rule of never discussing business during meals, holding forth on the various reasons New York had become the largest and most important city in the country and why it would likely stay that way for decades, if not centuries, to come. As usual, I mainly nodded, listened, and chewed, having nothing significant to add.

After dinner, we had coffee in the office, but there was little conversation, as Wolfe immersed himself in his latest book, *My Three Years in Moscow* by Walter Bedell Smith. At eight-twenty, I rose and announced I was off to the Lower East Side, but got no reaction from the man who signs my checks. A fascinating book, no doubt. A light drizzle had begun to fall, so I grabbed my raincoat from the hall rack and headed for Ninth Avenue to hail a southbound cab. Twenty-five minutes later, I found myself at the corner of Second Avenue and Sixth Street.

I spotted Mason's Book Nook, a narrow storefront whose cheerful inside lighting was a welcome contrast to the closed and darkened establishments on either side. When I stepped in, a little bell over the door announced my arrival. A man at the cash register with no hair on his head but plenty on his upper lip peered over half-glasses at me and smiled. "Welcome to Mason's," he said. "If we haven't got what you want, we'll do our darndest to get it. Just tell us how might we help you, young fella?"

"Just by calling me 'young fella' you have lifted my spirits,"

I told him, shaking the raindrops off my coat. "I'm looking for Miss Marlene Peters. I believe she is expecting me."

He threw me a suspicious look but quickly erased it. "Marlene!" he called, "A gentleman here to see you. At least I hope he's a gentleman," he added, winking at me to show that he sensed I was all right.

A short, slim redhead with a turned-up nose wearing a skirt, sweater, and large tortoise shell glasses emerged from the shadowy bowels of the store and fixed me with an expression somewhere between curious and cautious.

"It's Mr. Goodwin, isn't it?" she said, cocking her head.

"That's me all right. Did you check me out with your friend Cordelia?"

A slight smile creased her face as she shook her head. "No, I really didn't think I had to, and you don't need to show me your license."

"That is reassuring," I said. "I know I'm a little early, so if you don't mind, I'll just browse around until closing time."

"Marlene, it's been a slow night," the bald man said, stroking his white mustache. "You might as well take off now; I can close up."

"Are you sure, Mr. Mason?"

"Absolutely, unless Mr. Goodwin here really does want to do some browsing, which I certainly would not object to."

"You know, my boss is a lover of Charles Dickens' work, and he is also a lover of handsome volumes," I told him. "Do you happen to have anything that might make a good birthday gift?"

Mason, whom I assumed to be the owner, rubbed his palms together and stood, a grin creasing his face. "I believe I may have just the thing, Mr. Goodwin," he said, heading toward the back of the store as Marlene Peters got her purse from under the counter and ran a comb though her hair. Mason returned holding a small book with a calfskin binding and gilt edging. "This is a limited-edition number of *Great Expectations* that is as well made as any Dickens volume I've seen come through here in years," he said. "It was printed in London about 1910. Here's what I can let you have it for," he said, naming a price. The amount was about what I normally spent on Wolfe's birthday gift, so we had ourselves a deal. Marlene wrapped the book in silver gift paper with a red ribbon while I paid Mason.

As we walked out, he said, "Marlene, why don't you tell Mr. Goodwin about some of the other treasures that we have here? Who knows, maybe we can make a regular customer of him."

"Your boss seems like a nice guy," I said as we walked along Second Avenue toward a coffee shop Marlene had suggested.

"He is; he's just wonderful to work for. His wife died about a year ago, and none of his children live anywhere near New York, so the shop is pretty much his whole life now."

"Have you been there for a long time?"

"Not at all, I began just a couple of months ago," she said as we entered the café. "I want to work for a publishing company, someday as an editor, I hope, and I've got a lot of résumés out. Mr. Mason knows that, but he agreed to hire me even if it's only for a short time. The girl who was there before left to go back to college, so he needed someone as a replacement. The pay is not great, but I enjoy the place, and it's close to where I live."

We settled into a booth, and I insisted that Marlene order dinner. "This is on me," I told her. "I dragooned you into seeing me, so the least I can do is to feed you for your trouble."

"*Dragooned*. What an unusual term," she said.

"It means something like *forced* or *coerced*. My boss, Nero Wolfe, has a huge vocabulary, and I've learned all sorts of words from him. Some of them I may even use correctly."

That got a laugh out of Marlene. "Are you going to have something to eat, too?" she asked.

"I've already had dinner, but to keep you company, I'll have a piece of pie and a glass of milk."

She ordered a steak sandwich with fries and tied into her meal as if she hadn't eaten in a week. I waited until she had finished before getting down to business. "Marlene, tell me about your trip to Florence."

"I had been in that city before, and on this vacation to Europe, the only place in Italy I had planned to visit was Rome. But when I learned that Cordelia was going to Florence for the first time, I thought it would be fun if we were there at the same time, at least for a week or so, and I ended up altering my plans."

"You had been classmates in college?"

"Yes, at Vassar. We lived in the same hall and got to know each other early on. And we've been friends ever since, five or six years now."

"Nice to have long-running friendships like that. Cordelia said you got together several times in Florence."

She nodded. "We did, sometimes just the two of us and sometimes with . . . well, with a man she had met."

"Really? An Italian?"

"Yes, his name is Carlo. He lives in Florence and comes from a very wealthy family in the leather business."

"Would you say this was a serious relationship?"

Marlene bit a lip. "I know they seemed to get along, but . . . how well do you know Cordelia?"

"Not very. I've only been with her a couple of times."

"I feel funny talking about a good friend like this, but Cordelia is really quite inexperienced with men, at least for someone her age."

"I was under the impression she had some sort of understanding with a man here in New York," I said, improvising.

"Lanny Mercer, yes. I haven't talked to Cordelia lately, but I know they were beginning to make plans. He seems like a nice fellow, based on the few times I've met him. His family owns a business that makes airplanes, mostly for private companies, I believe."

"Do you feel her meeting this Carlo in Florence has had an effect on that relationship?"

"I just don't know, Mr. Goodwin." She frowned and shook her head.

"Well, do you think it is possible that the blackmailing has anything to do with this Carlo? And further, has Cordelia stayed in touch with him since she's been back home?"

Marlene ran a hand through her hair. "I wish I could answer your questions, but I haven't talked to Cordelia in a few weeks now. I've called her for lunch a couple of times, but she's always been busy. And she seems very distracted over the telephone, maybe because of this blackmailing business that you're talking about."

"Maybe, but she refuses to get specific about it," I said. "Her father, who hired us, knew something was bothering her and pushed her to tell him what it is. She finally did admit she was being blackmailed but would say nothing more about it. So it is up to us to figure out what's going on."

"Poor Cordelia. I wish there was something I could do for her."

"You know her brother, Doug, don't you?"

"Well, yes, in a way," she said. "Cordelia thought we would get along well and introduced us. We went out a few times a while back, but it just didn't click, maybe because he's quite a bit older than I am."

"So you don't see him anymore?"

She shook her head. "That is all in the past for me."

"Anything else you can think of that might help us understand what's going on with Cordelia?"

"As I said when you telephoned me, Mr. Goodwin, I really don't think so. What I will do is call Cordelia again for lunch. Perhaps something will come of that."

"Please let me know if you learn something that is of interest." I gave her my business card.

"I will, as long as I am not betraying any confidences. And thank you very much for dinner," Marlene said, sliding out of the booth and moving toward the door.

"I would be happy to walk you home," I said, but she told me she lived less than two blocks away. She seemed to be in a hurry to leave, and I was not about to slow her down.

CHAPTER 22

After breakfast the next morning, I welcomed a very attractive visitor—but don't go getting any ideas. Doc Vollmer's comely nurse, Carol Francis, had come to remove the last of my bandages, or so I hoped. My teres minor appeared to have healed, and now I could raise my left arm as high as ever—and most importantly, without pain.

We went up to my room, where I stripped to the waist. Carol—we were now on a first-name basis—began pulling off the tape I had been swathed in several times since the shooting.

"I wonder what my dear friend Lily would say if she could see us now?" I asked Carol.

"She would say you are one lucky fellow to have such a capable nurse looking after you, Archie," she said as she unwrapped me. "And she would also congratulate you on having such good recuperative powers."

"Does that mean no more bandaging?"

"Not quite, big guy. I am going to wrap you up once more, but with less tape this time. We want to make sure the healing is complete. Based on what I've seen, two more weeks should do it, maximum, and I'll come back for one session. You will be glad to see the last of me."

"That is where you are wrong. I'll miss your visits."

"Hah, so you say, you sweet-talker. I know better. I have seen how you grimace each time I pull off the tape and rewrap you," Carol said.

"I guess I'm just a big sissy."

"Sissy? I really don't think so. Not from what I have heard about your exploits."

"Just who have you been talking to? I'll bet it was your boss, that rascal Doc Vollmer."

"My lips are sealed. Now, you behave yourself and stay out of the line of fire in the future. It's not healthy, do you hear?"

"Yes, Nurse. I hereby promise to be more careful."

She rose to leave, and as she walked out of my room, she looked back over her shoulder and winked. I winked back, of course.

I got dressed and went down to the office to go through the morning mail. One thing was puzzling me that I had put out of my mind over the last couple of days. Ever since Saul Panzer had dinner with Wolfe when I was out breaking bread with Annie Hutchinson, I hadn't heard anything from him. This was unusual, as we normally talked nearly every day, even when he wasn't doing a job for us. Even more unusual was Fred Durkin's call to tell me that our weekly poker game at Saul's had been canceled.

"That is strange, given that he usually takes our money," I told Fred. "Is our host ill?"

"I don't know, Archie. He just phoned me and asked that I tell the rest of you the game was off for this week."

As I mentioned earlier, Wolfe often gives Saul an assignment without bothering to inform me. Was this one of those times? I could ask, of course, but as has happened in the past, I likely would not get a straight answer from him.

When Wolfe came down from the plant rooms at eleven and got settled in the reinforced chair behind his desk, I swiveled to face him. "I now have completed interviews with all of the principals in the Hutchinson case," I told him.

"All but one," he contradicted.

"Okay, who am I missing? I will get on it pronto."

"That is not necessary, Archie. It is being taken care of."

The little alarm bell that went off in my brain sent me the message that Saul Panzer was in some way involved, but I couldn't figure out how, and I was damned if I was going to ask. Instead, I said to Wolfe, "Sounds like you have everything well in hand at the moment. If you don't have need for me the rest of the day, as seems apparent, I thought I might go out to the Giants game at the Polo Grounds this afternoon. It is a beautiful day, and the Cardinals are in town with the great Stan Musial, who is currently batting almost .400. And it is fair to say I'm owed the time off, given all the evenings that I have been working lately. Unless, of course, you think otherwise."

"Archie, fits of pique do not become you. I realize you are eager to disencumber yourself of the information you have amassed, and I am eager to hear it. But haste is the enemy of the judicious. Let us discuss the matter after dinner. Go, enjoy the baseball game."

In fact, I did enjoy the game, even though the Giants got their ears boxed by a very good St. Louis team led by the superb Musial, who hit a home run and two doubles and drove in five runs, which was more than the entire New York team scored.

I got back home before Wolfe's descent from the plant rooms, which gave me time to mentally review all of the meetings I'd had with members of the Hutchinson clan and Marlene Peters. Following a dinner of squabs with sausage and sauerkraut, during which Wolfe extolled the essays of Montaigne, particularly his "Of the Education of Children," we moved into the office for coffee. Since he makes it clear that he runs the show, I waited for him to say he was ready to hear from me. He finished his second cup of coffee, rang for beer, and set down that day's *Times* crossword puzzle, which he had, as usual, completed. "Report," he said.

"Yes, sir." I proceeded to give him my interviews in the order I had conducted them. As is my practice, I unloaded them to him verbatim, including hesitations, inflections, and pregnant pauses on the part of the interviewees. The business took more than an hour and a half, during which time Wolfe alternated between drinking beer and leaning back with hands interlaced over his middle mound. "That is the whole of it," I told him when I had finished. "What do you think?"

I got no answer and looked over at Wolfe, seeing why. He was leaning back, but this time with eyes closed and with his lips pushing in and out, in and out. I knew he was in a place where I couldn't reach him; nobody could. Being one who likes to keep statistics at baseball games and séances, I checked my watch and waited. Forty-three minutes later, Wolfe opened his eyes and blinked twice.

"Bah! I have been a consummate lackwit," he said. "The answer was as plain as an elephant's trunk, there before me, but I was too thickheaded to realize it. My private investigator's license should be revoked by the state on the grounds of gross ineptitude."

"If you are done flagellating yourself, would you deign to share your discovery with me?" I asked.

He did, slowly and thoroughly, and everything made perfect sense, complicated as it was. You may have figured out at least part of the puzzle by this time, but I had barely gotten beyond first base.

"What do we do now?"

Wolfe drew in his usual bushel of air and exhaled. "You will call them—every one—and have them here."

"When, pray tell?"

"Day after tomorrow, nine in the evening."

"Why not sooner?"

"I have reasons," he said, "that need not trouble you at the moment."

"Okay, I'll let that one pass, since you love to have your little secrets. You will concede that I have been pretty successful over the years in rounding up people for your gatherings here. I'm not as confident this time in being able to rope in all the members of the Hutchinson clan."

"I believe you can, Archie. You can tell them that we will lift the burden that Miss Hutchinson has been carrying, and that it is vital they all be here—and I include Miss Peters—to better understand the circumstances of Miss Hutchinson's plight."

"I assume no mention should be made of the gunplay in Central Park and the death of Alan Marx."

"Your assumption is correct. However, when I call Inspector Cramer, my selling point to him will be the murders."

"Should I invite Saul to join me in hosting the festivities?"

"That will not be necessary. I have made arrangements for Saul to be present," he said.

"And, of course, the reason for his presence should not trouble me?"

Of course," Wolfe replied.

CHAPTER 23

As I had feared, it was no picnic trying to bring everybody in for Wolfe's little party. I started with our client, and even he balked initially. "I do not know why I can't just come over there and meet with Wolfe alone," Parkhurst Hutchinson said in a tone that indicated he was used to getting his way. He was reverting to his bullying ways.

"This is not how Mr. Wolfe works," I told him. "You have hired him for his brains, but in the deal you also get his eccentricities, which I concede are considerable." The railroad tycoon was not satisfied, and we went back and forth for several minutes before I finally wore him down.

"All right, dammit. I suppose my wife should be along as well?"

"Yes, she should, and Cordelia, of course."

"Who else will be present?"

"We are inviting all of your children, and also Cordelia's friend, Marlene Peters."

"Is this really necessary, Goodwin? As I see it, the embarrassment to Cordelia will be acute."

"I am afraid some others may also be embarrassed, sir," I said.

"What can you tell me about the program?"

"Nothing, as I don't really know what Mr. Wolfe is planning," I lied. "Other than to say there will be no further attempts to blackmail Cordelia, and that the blackmailer will be revealed, which should be a relief to everyone."

"Well, at least that is something," Hutchinson huffed.

"I believe that was the commission we were charged with," I told him coldly.

He huffed again and our conversation concluded. Of the clan other than Cordelia, none seemed anxious to come to the brownstone. Annie tried to beg off, claiming another engagement. "Is it really necessary that I be there?" she asked plaintively.

"Your parents and all your siblings will be present. Your absence would be noted, certainly by your parents."

That got me a grumble and a reluctant acceptance. Brother Tom was an only slightly easier sell. "I don't see what I could possibly contribute by being there," he said. "You know everything I do. I unloaded it all when we had lunch."

"Mr. Wolfe seems to think it is important that the whole family be there to present a united front in support of Cordelia," I improvised. "I don't have to tell you that she has been through a really rough time."

"Oh, all right, I surrender," he sighed. "Can you give me directions? I'll show up and try to behave myself."

Doug was a tough sell once I finally reached him. "I'm not sure what all this is supposed to prove," he muttered. "I'm in the middle of working on a new oil, and I hate any kind of interruption when I'm doing well. What's more, I've got a commission on this one—a chance to make some honest-to-goodness shekels for a change."

"You're only being asked to give an hour or so on one night. I am sure your youngest sister would appreciate the support."

"Frankly, Mr. Goodwin, my youngest sister won't give two hoots whether I'm there or not."

"However, it would not look good if you were the only absent Hutchinson," I persisted.

"Anybody besides the family going to be there?"

"No," I said, following Wolfe's orders.

"Oh, screw it, I'll show up," he groused before hanging up on me. Fortunately, I had already given him our address. I hoped he would remember it.

Kathleen started by grumbling about the idea of coming into the city at night. "I really try to avoid New York these days, Archie," she said. "Part of the reason is that I have to get a babysitter for my girls whenever I go into town."

"Can't their father do the honors that night?"

"Oh God, trying to get him to help with any parenting beyond what we worked out in the settlement is like trying to push a peanut down the street with your nose. What time do you think the session at your boss's place will be over?"

"I'm hoping by ten—ten thirty at the latest."

"Okay . . . Here's what I think I can do: I've got a neighbor, a really swell gal, whose own little girl stayed overnight with us when my neighbor had an emergency, so I will see if she can reciprocate." I told her that was a good idea and gave her the address of the brownstone.

Next, I called Marlene Peters. After getting no answer at her apartment, I tried the bookstore, with success. I had less success in getting her to agree to come to West Thirty-Fifth Street. "No, do not count me in," she said sternly. "I don't see how my being there would help in any way."

"I gather you haven't called Cordelia again about having lunch."

"Uh, no, I haven't. But I'm going to, in the next few days for sure."

"Then you may not know that she specifically asked for you to be there for support," I said, wondering how many lies I could get away with before one of them caught up with me.

"Who else is going to be there?" she asked.

"I'm not sure yet. Besides Cordelia, probably only her parents, her brother Tom, and maybe her sister Annie." Yet another lie. I was definitely headed for Hades.

"Will you be there, too?"

"Yes, but only as an observer. This is Nero Wolfe's show."

"Exactly what does that mean?"

"It means he will try his best to show Cordelia's parents that their daughter has been the innocent victim of someone in Italy."

"I hope he succeeds," she said, sounding as if she meant it. "All right, if only for Cordelia's sake, I will be there."

When Wolfe came down from the plant rooms at eleven and got himself settled, I grinned. "You don't pay me enough for this type of work, but then you already know that. I talked to the whole guest list this morning, and they will all be here tomorrow night. At least they say they will. Never mind what I had to tell some of them to get them here."

"Satisfactory. Get Inspector Cramer."

I dialed a number I knew by heart as Wolfe picked up his instrument and I stayed on the line. As is usually the case, Cramer picked up the phone himself, barking his last name.

"Inspector, this is Nero Wolfe."

"Yeah, somehow I recognize the voice. Why do I want to talk to you?"

"Tomorrow night, I am going to identify two murderers: the individual who shot Noah McManus in Central Park and the one who killed Alan Marx with a fireplace poker in his home."

"Whoa, slow down. Who is your client? You always have one, usually rich, very rich. I have never known you to take on charity cases."

"My client will become apparent to you tomorrow. You may come if you wish, and you may want to bring Sergeant Stebbins with you."

"Are you trying to tell me my business?"

"Far be it from me to do such a thing, Inspector. I am simply extending a courtesy to you."

"Courtesy, hah! You sound to me like you're showing off—yet again."

"Whether or not I am 'showing off,' to use your phrase," Wolfe said, "it is you who will be credited with making an arrest in a highly publicized case."

"If an arrest is actually made," Cramer snorted.

"The choice is yours, sir. Tomorrow evening at nine, a number of individuals will be gathered here."

"Care to name them?"

"I do not."

"You are dealing with a police matter here, Wolfe."

"Inspector, do you have any leads as to the shooting death in Central Park? Or the killing of Alan Marx?" Cramer's answer was one of those words no so-called "family newspaper" would print.

"I can be of help to you, sir, and to the department as well. The decision remains yours. Good day." Wolfe and I cradled our instruments. "You are fond of giving odds, Archie," he said. "What are the odds the inspector will be with us here tomorrow night?"

"Ten to one, in favor," I answered. "I give the same odds that Purley Stebbins will be with him."

"As do I. I would have put forth eight to one, but I yield to your instincts involving probabilities."

"Cramer simply cannot afford to stay away and you know it," I said. "The stakes are too high and the pressure on the department is too great. He knows damned well that if you really do have information about these killings—which of course you do—he runs the risk of learning about it secondhand in the pages of our old friend Lon Cohen's newspaper, *The Gazette*—which, as Lon loves to remind us, has the fifth-largest circulation of any daily journal in the land of the free and the home of the brave. End of sermon."

Wolfe allowed himself a look of satisfaction and rang for beer. I felt pretty satisfied myself, although I was beginning to get a case of nerves, which always happens to me when we have one of these wingdings.

Not so with Wolfe, who seems to thrive on the drama and the tension. But then, he's the stage manager and has full control of the production.

CHAPTER 24

Fritz has always been able to read my moods, and it did not take him long the next morning to realize I was on edge. As he served me the next in a series of buttermilk wheat cakes hot off the griddle, he fixed me with a concerned look. "You are having an important meeting tonight?"

"We are. But not to worry, I do not think it will erupt into a brawl. Besides, the police will be represented at this little gathering in the form of Messrs. Cramer and Stebbins."

He still looked concerned, but then, Fritz is almost always concerned. When Wolfe has a case, he worries that his boss might be working too hard—which is enough to make me laugh. He worries when we don't have a case because no money is coming in. He worries whenever I leave the brownstone on business because something might happen to me. Imagine how much he has been worrying about me lately, given what has happened to yours truly!

I tried to put him at ease, although without success. After all, I was hardly a model of tranquility myself. I spent the rest of the day puttering and trying to keep my mind off the impending showdown. I entered orchid germination records left on my desk by Theodore Horstmann, typed a half-dozen letters Wolfe had dictated the day before, paid the grocery and beer bills, balanced the checkbook, and took an armful of my shirts to the cleaners over on Eighth Avenue.

As much as I enjoy Fritz's cooking, I barely remember the details of either lunch or dinner that day, although I would never admit it to him. At eight o'clock, I was setting up chairs in the office when the doorbell rang.

"Lord," I said to myself, "it must be Cramer, coming early to demand to know what's going on. But when I looked through the one-way glass, I got a surprise.

I swung open the front door and faced a smiling Saul Panzer, who was not alone. "Evening, Archie," Saul said, "I would like you to meet Carlo Veronese, of whom you may have heard." The other man on the stoop was at least ten years younger and six inches taller than Saul. He was also far better clothed, in a silk, pin striped navy-blue suit, and was obviously ill at ease.

"Nice to meet you," I said, shaking the Italian's hand.

"Thank you, a pleasure, *signore*," he said in heavily accented but understandable English, forcing a smile.

"Mr. Wolfe thought Mr. Veronese and I should wait in the front room until such time as he calls us into the meeting. I can get us both something to drink." He turned to Veronese, asking what he would like. The young man, a square-shouldered, handsome specimen with wavy black hair and chiseled features, shyly asked for red wine. Saul gestured him to the front room and closed the door behind him.

"All right, fill me in," I said to Saul as we walked down the hall to the office. "What gives?"

"I'm sorry about canceling the poker game, but Mr. Wolfe

sent me to Italy—Florence, to be specific—to get young Mr. Veronese and bring him here."

"Interesting. I should have figured that out. Did you have a tough sell getting him to agree?"

Saul gave me a crooked smile. "Yes, at first, but I can be quite persuasive. I pointed out to him that he might well be an accessory to a crime—specifically blackmail—and that if he came to the States, he could plead his case and have a far better chance of getting cleared, rather than having to face a courtroom in Florence, where the Tuscan authorities have recently been handing down longer jail sentences to Italian men who beguile and often debauch young female tourists, mainly from the US, Canada, England, Holland, and Germany—many of them blondes. I told him Mr. Wolfe would cast him in a sympathetic light."

"When did you fly in?"

"Around noon. We are both more than a little bleary-eyed, and young Veronese is extremely nervous, as you could see," Saul said. "He's actually been in the States once before, to visit relatives in Philadelphia, and he has traveled to most of the other European countries, too. As you know, there's lots of money in his family, old money."

"So I've heard tell. Well, as long as he's here, let's show him American hospitality. Get him his drink, and have one yourself from the cart. I'm just setting up for tonight's show, as you can see."

"Is it safe to assume Cramer will be here?"

"Very safe, and with Stebbins in his shadow."

"Of course. How are you feeling, Archie?"

"Shoulder's almost back to normal," I said, flexing it. "Grab your drinks, and I'll see you later in the evening. Should be interesting."

Tom Hutchinson was the first one to arrive, at ten till nine.

"Archie, good to see you again," he said, pumping my hand. "I really did enjoy that lunch we had. I would be glad to reciprocate some time.

"Oh, my," he said as he stepped into the office, "it looks like you're all set up for a show."

"That's a good way to put it," I said as the doorbell rang again. "Help yourself to something liquid." I gestured toward the cart. "I've stocked it with everything I could think that people might want."

I opened the door to Cramer and Stebbins, neither of whom looked happy. No surprise there. "Where's Wolfe?" the inspector barked, surging by me and heading down the hall.

"He's not in his office yet," I called after him. Stebbins followed in his wake after scowling at me, as he has been doing for years. I scowled back, as I have been doing for years also.

I turned toward the still-open door to see that Mr. and Mrs. Parkhurst Hutchinson and Cordelia were climbing the steps. They looked no happier than Cramer and Stebbins. "Who were those men who arrived just ahead of us?" Hutchinson demanded. "I've never seen them before. Why are they here? Are they newspapermen?"

"You will know soon enough," I replied. "Please come this way." I smiled at Mrs. Hutchinson, whom I had not met, and got a blank stare in return. She was barely five feet, and very thin, with a pinched face and a disapproving expression that appeared to be a permanent condition. I realized I did not even know her first name.

Cordelia looked up at me, smiling weakly but saying nothing. I knew she was going through her own version of hell, but I also knew the worst was yet to come. I got father, mother, and son Tom seated in the first row of chairs in front of Wolfe's desk before the bell rang once more. The two female siblings arrived together, whether by design or coincidence. Annie gave me a tight smile while Kathleen rolled her eyes and shrugged, as if to say, "Well, you talked me into coming here tonight, now what?"

While I was getting them seated in the back row of chairs, the bell chimed once more. Fritz did the honors this time, and as I stepped out into the hall, I saw that he was welcoming Doug at the door. The younger brother looked even less happy to be here than the others, but I was pleased to see him, figuring that with his attitude, he might well have been a no-show. No sooner did I take over from Fritz and escort the dour artist into the office than our final guest, Marlene Peters, arrived. She said something to Fritz that I didn't catch, and she gave me an expressionless nod of recognition as she came toward me, but said nothing.

I steered her into the office and observed a variety of reactions to her presence: The elder Hutchinsons each looked surprised; Cordelia fluttered a hand in what I took to be a small wave; Annie pursed her lips in disapproval; and Doug stiffened, making me suspect their parting had not been an amicable one. Marlene herself tensed up when she saw him.

I offered drinks to the assemblage but did not get many takers. Papa Hutchinson asked for his usual scotch on the rocks and Annie requested a white wine. All of the others declined. Everyone was in place now. Cordelia, as the client, at least nominally, had the place of honor in the red leather chair this time, displacing her father. The senior Hutchinsons and Tom occupied the first row as previously noted, and Annie, Doug, Kathleen, and Marlene were in the row behind them. As is usual in these sessions, Cramer and Stebbins stood grim faced, their backs against the wall behind the others.

"Just where is Mr. Wolfe?" Parkhurst Hutchinson demanded, looking around. He was reverting to his earlier curmudgeonly mode.

"He will be here momentarily," I said, going behind his desk and pushing the buzzer, which sounded in the kitchen. He had been parked there for the last half hour, waiting to make his grand entrance.

"Good evening," Wolfe said as he entered the room and detoured around his desk, sitting and observing his guests. "I presume you have all been offered refreshments. I am going to have beer." He then surveyed the audience again, calling each of them by name.

"All right, you got everyone here and you know our names. I fail to be impressed by that," Parkhurst Hutchinson said. "But I notice you did not identify those two men in the back. I already asked Goodwin who they are, and I did not get a straight answer from him."

Wolfe dipped his chin as Fritz brought the beer in. "They are Inspector Cramer of the New York Police Department's Homicide Division and his associate, Sergeant Stebbins. They are here at my invitation."

"Why, for God's sake?" Hutchinson barked as his wife put a hand on his arm, trying to quiet him. "Is this going to turn into some sort of kangaroo court?"

"It is not, sir," Wolfe said calmly. "But as the evening progresses, I assure you, the need for their presence will become apparent."

CHAPTER 25

If Wolfe's statement was intended to get their attention, it did the trick. Everyone started talking at once, although the booming voice of the railroad titan quickly overwhelmed the others.

"Just what do you mean by saying that?" Parkhurst Hutchinson demanded. "I thought we were here because of a blackmailing. Yet these men investigate homicides, don't they?" he said, gesturing with a thumb toward Cramer and Stebbins.

"This case goes well beyond blackmailing," Wolfe said. "If you will be patient, I shall reconstruct the events that led us to be together tonight. First, I must offer an apology."

"What for?" Doug blurted out. "For dragging us here when we'd all rather be someplace else?"

Wolfe ignored the young artist. "I apologize for not identifying the complexities of this case more quickly. What I originally determined to be two discrete concernments were inextricably bound together. I should have realized this far sooner. For that, I stand chagrined."

"Pretty fancy talk," Annie Hutchinson said. "Do you think you can make it clearer for us simple folk?"

"I shall endeavor to do so. The plotting, if it can be so termed, was ill-designed and convoluted, with so many elements and moving parts that it eventually collapsed under its own weight."

"Just what are these two discrete concernments?" Tom Hutchinson asked. "You lost me there, and I suspect you lost some others as well, unless I am particularly dense, which of course is possible."

Wolfe drank beer and dabbed his lips with a handkerchief. "There was the blackmailing, of course, and there also was a plan afoot to kill Mr. Goodwin, which came perilously close to succeeding." Wolfe turned to me with an expression that was the closest thing to affection I had ever seen from him.

His comment got the assemblage riled up again, as every face in the room turned toward me with varying expressions of shock and amazement.

"You had better explain that," Cramer said, "and do it very thoroughly."

"As you are well aware, Inspector, I have made numerous enemies over the years. One of these individuals came out of the woodwork recently, both with verbal threats delivered by telephone and with apparent attempts upon Mr. Goodwin's life as a way to get revenge against me."

"The gunshots from a car fired on this block one night, and the bullet holes in your front windows," Cramer supplied.

"Yes, and some time later, as I will get into, a gunshot fired at point-blank range that Mr. Goodwin barely survived."

"I want to know right now what—"

Wolfe held up a hand. "Later, Inspector. First the blackmailing, which Mr. Hutchinson has commissioned me to investigate. Cordelia Hutchinson received telephone calls, letters, and a seemingly incriminating photograph. The caller said that if Miss Hutchinson did not pay a sizable amount, in cash, the photograph would be made public."

"The son of a bitch," Tom said.

"Perhaps. Miss Hutchinson came to me with the notes and the photograph, saying she knew of my reputation and wanted me to get the other copies of the photograph back, even though it meant paying the money."

"This was a job for the police," Cramer snorted.

"I suggested that to her, but she strongly demurred."

"You should have insisted!"

"Mr. Cramer, let us have this discussion at another time. Miss Hutchinson, am I correct that you did not recognize the caller's voice?"

"Correct, I didn't recognize it," Cordelia said, after clearing her throat.

"She also told me the incriminating photograph came to her by mail," Wolfe said. "I believe this. However, I also believe that the blackmail notes, which I have, were created by Miss Hutchinson herself."

"What! Are you out of your mind?" It was Cordelia's father, who came halfway out of his chair.

"I believe my sanity to be intact, thank you," Wolfe said. "When Miss Hutchinson brought us the notes, both printed in ink with block letters, I asked about the envelopes, which she said she had thrown away."

"What of it?" Kathleen asked.

"Come now, Mrs. Willis. Would anyone who has received a blackmail letter—and kept it—throw away the envelope it came in? That goes against the very essence of human nature. If for no other reason, an envelope would instinctively be saved in part for any evidence of the sender's identity it might provide—such as fingerprints. There were never any envelopes."

Cordelia was staring at her lap and vigorously twisting a hanky. Her parents both looked at her, but she kept her head down.

"Does this mean Miss Hutchinson planned her own blackmailing? It does not," Wolfe said, answering his own question and flipping a palm. "However, it does indicate the thrall in which she was held by the telephone caller and her terror at the photograph being made public. This individual also told her—perhaps insisted—that she should engage me to have the ransom money delivered to a specified location."

Annie Hutchinson raised her hand like a pupil in a classroom and Wolfe nodded toward her.

"Just a minute," she said. "How did this phone caller know you would even accept the assignment?"

"A very good question. The caller was taking a chance on my acceding to Cordelia Hutchinson's request that we stop the blackmailer, but not necessarily identify him or her."

"But were you planning to identify him or her?" Annie persisted, leaning forward in her chair.

"We had made provisions for that."

"One last question, Mr. Wolfe, and then I'll shut up," Annie said. "Of all the detectives in New York, and there must be dozens, why were you selected by the blackmailer?"

"Another excellent query. Now we arrive at the confluence of our two metaphorical rivers: the blackmailing and the plot against Mr. Goodwin. There were two interests here, and these interests did their planning in concert.

"It probably began with a chance meeting months ago between two individuals, each with a goal. One sought a substantial sum of money to improve a standard of living, the other sought revenge upon me through Mr. Goodwin. Each party felt he or she had hit upon a way to accomplish both ends."

"Let us get on with the blackmailing," Parkhurst Hutchinson grumped. "After all, that is what we are paying you for."

"Let us indeed, sir," Wolfe replied amiably. "Your daughter had planned a trip earlier this year to Italy as she told me, one that was to include many cities and attractions throughout that country. Her first stop was Florence, and something occurred there that made her drastically alter her itinerary."

"A man!" her father said.

"Yes, a man named Carlo Veronese, from a wealthy and well-established Florentine family. Is that not correct, Miss Hutchinson?"

Cordelia looked up and nodded, then dropped her head back down again. I was almost feeling sorry for her.

"You met Mr. Veronese, seemingly by chance, while you were window shopping on the Ponte Vecchio Bridge, is that also correct?"

"It *was* by chance," she said in a voice just above a whisper.

"I think not," Wolfe replied, pushing the buzzer under his desk. "I believe the meeting was carefully planned."

"Not by me!" Cordelia squeaked.

"No, not by you," Wolfe agreed as the door opened and Saul Panzer and Carlo Veronese stepped in. Cordelia gasped, as did Marlene Peters.

"Good evening Mr. Veronese," Wolfe said, not inviting him to be seated. "Thank you for coming. Do you recognize some of the people here?"

"Two," Carlo said, abashed. He gave a tight smile to Cordelia and avoided looking at Marlene.

"Tell us how you happened to meet Miss Hutchinson in Florence earlier this year."

"She was . . . identified to me, I would say."

"By whom, Mr. Veronese?"

"By . . . her," he said, pointing at Marlene, who started to say something but changed her mind. Like Cordelia, she was looking down.

"Miss Peters," Wolfe stated. "Had you known her previously?"

Veronese nodded. "We met last year."

"Would you say you were good friends?"

"Mm, yes, good friends, but not . . ." He made hand gestures that I took to mean the two had not been lovers.

"Why did Miss Peters want you to meet Miss Hutchinson?" Wolfe posed.

Veronese shifted from one leg to the other, clearly uncomfortable with the grilling he was getting. "She said it would help to make her boyfriend back at home . . . what is the word—*jealous*?"

"Why should Miss Hutchinson want him to be jealous?"

"Marlene . . . Miss Peters said it would get him to make what you call a proposal to her."

"That's not true! Lanny had already proposed to me, and you knew it!" Cordelia cried, glowering at Marlene. "How dare you . . ."

"Photographs of you and Miss Hutchinson were taken in the Boboli Gardens," Wolfe said to Veronese. "You knew about that, of course." The Italian nodded, hanging his head.

"And you also arranged for a photographer to take those pictures, a *paparazzo*? Did Miss Peters help you with that?" Another nod.

Wolfe looked at Marlene. "It's . . . just . . . it's not what it sounds like," she mumbled. "I . . . don't want to say any more right now."

"I understand you and Douglas Hutchinson have spent time together," Wolfe said. Doug shifted in his chair.

"Well, we did go out a few times, a while back," she responded.

"Yes, and you and he are still keeping company, aren't you?"

"What? No, I mean, I really don't see where this is any of . . ." Marlene's voice trailed off, and she began crying. By this time, Cordelia was sobbing, too, for different reasons. I just hoped Wolfe could hold up. He detests female emotions, and we had more than enough of them in the room, especially since Cordelia's mother had begun shedding tears quietly.

Wolfe stayed focused on Marlene. "When Mr. Goodwin asked you about this relationship, you said 'it just didn't click.' And when the same question was asked of Douglas, he used precisely the same words, as if the two of you had been expecting the question and had done some rehearsing. What about it, Mr. Hutchinson?" Wolfe said, turning to Doug.

"That was just a coincidence," he said dismissively, throwing his arms up. "We haven't been together in ages."

Back to Marlene. "Is it true what he says, Miss Peters, that you haven't been together in ages?" Wolfe was attacking the weakest point in the pair, and he did not let her sniffling deter him.

"Oh for God's sake, leave her alone!" Doug barked and stood. "I'm getting out of here."

"Not just yet you aren't, son," Purley Stebbins said, stepping forward and putting one of his oversized paws on the young man's shoulder, forcing him back down into his chair.

"So, let us leave this couple for the moment and go back to the beginning of this chain of events," Wolfe said. "A few minutes ago, I spoke of a chance meeting between two individuals, whom

I shall call X and Y. Each had a specific goal. They saw how they could aid each other in achieving these goals.

"Their plan, while flawed, appealed to both of them. The person intent upon killing Mr. Goodwin was also the telephone voice of the blackmailer, a voice unknown to Miss Hutchinson. This person, X, sent one of the photographs taken in Florence to her, demanding seventy-five thousand dollars in currency in return for the other photographs. X dictated the content of two ransom notes to her, undoubtedly suggesting she print them to avoid a handwriting test.

"X then stipulated that she attempt to hire us to deliver the money to a specified spot in Central Park, knowing that if we did accept the assignment, Mr. Goodwin would almost surely be the one making the delivery, as I am patently unsuited to such work. If all went well, Mr. Goodwin would be dead and the money would go to the other member of the cabal, Y. The one final thing that did go well for X and Y is that we accepted the assignment from Miss Hutchinson, who was totally ignorant of both the death plot and the ultimate destination of the seventy-five thousand dollars."

"This plan sounds awfully convoluted, to use one of your own words," Cramer said. "I don't see how in hell it could work."

"It did not work, Inspector, although Mr. Goodwin came close to losing his life. He did indeed take the satchel of money, seventy-five thousand dollars' worth, to the specified spot in Central Park, although he was not alone. To use a police term, he had backup, including Mr. Saul Panzer, whom you see there standing next to Mr. Veronese.

"X, who wanted my colleague dead, made the mistake of hiring a petty and inept mobster named Noah McManus to do the killing. When Mr. Goodwin set the satchel down at the base of a tree and began to walk away, McManus called out to him. Mr.

Goodwin turned and a bullet that should have killed him tore through his shoulder, knocking him to the ground. A moment later, the would-be assassin was shot in the back, fatally.

"I believe that X, thinking Mr. Goodwin was now dead, did what he had intended to do all along, which was to kill McManus, who was probably the only person who knew X was behind the planned killing. As Mr. Goodwin lay on the ground in pain, McManus prepared to fire a second and probably fatal shot at him, but unintentionally and ironically, X saved the very life he had sought to end."

CHAPTER 26

After that recitation, a hush fell over the room for several seconds. Once more, to my discomfort, I became the center of attention, as everyone stared at me, several of them agape, perhaps in surprise because I was alive. Finally, Tom Hutchinson broke the silence. "I'm sure glad you're okay, Archie, but I've got a question which might seem unimportant after all that happened in Central Park. What became of the money?"

"Your youngest sister could answer that for you," Wolfe said. "It has been returned to her. In the ensuing chaos after the melee in the park, another one of my agents, Fred Durkin, scooped up the satchel before either X or Y could retrieve it. It was returned to Miss Hutchinson intact."

"And just how did Goodwin get patched up?" Cramer demanded. "Gunshot wounds have to be reported."

"You and I can discuss this later, Mr. Cramer. There's more to tell about X and Y. Needless to say, neither of them was happy about the debacle in Central Park that made so many headlines, upset our civic leaders, and gave fodder to newspaper editorial writers."

"One more thing," Cramer said. "How do we know that either Panzer here or Durkin didn't fire the shot that killed McManus?"

"It is true that both were armed, but neither of them ever fired his weapon," Wolfe said. "You can put them on the witness stand or give them lie-detector tests."

Cramer looked unconvinced. "You claim McManus told no one else about the plan to kill Goodwin. What about the one you insist on calling Y?"

"Y did not know that killing Mr. Goodwin was part of the plan and was angered by everything that happened in the park. Y later confronted X and a struggle broke out in which X was killed."

"Okay, it's time to put names with these letters," Cramer said. "Or do you even know the names?"

"I do, sir. X, as you may have surmised, was Alan Marx, the man who was found dead recently in his Upper East Side residence, having been bludgeoned with a fireplace poker."

Cramer nodded. "The brother of Simeon Marx, who strangled that dancer and who you helped send to the chair."

"The selfsame. He detested me, and by extension, Mr. Goodwin. I am sure, beyond a reasonable doubt, that Alan Marx was the voice at the other end of the doomsaying telephone calls we received, and was responsible for the shots fired at Mr. Goodwin out on Thirty-Fifth Street and into our front-room windows. I also think it likely that Mr. McManus was the gunman in both of those cases. Of course, now we will never know."

"So that leaves the one you call 'Y.'"

"Yes, Inspector. He is in this room," Wolfe said, fixing his gaze on Douglas Hutchinson as Purley Stebbins moved behind him.

Doug spun around, feeling Stebbins's strong hand once again on his shoulder. "What the hell are you talking about, fat man?" he blurted. "You don't know what you're saying."

"Of all the Hutchinsons, you are the one most in need of money," Wolfe said, "and your youngest sister presently has the most readily available capital of any of your siblings. She looked to be easy pickings for you and your longtime friend Miss Peters here."

"My God, this is preposterous!" Parkhurst Hutchinson barked, bounding to his feet and turning toward his son. "Tell me that Nero Wolfe is out of his mind, dammit. Tell me!"

Stone-faced, Doug looked up at his father, saying nothing. Sweat broke out on his brow, and any resistance seemed to have left him.

"Douglas Hutchinson, appalled by the violence in Central Park and irate because of his failure to get the seventy-five thousand dollars, went to Marx's home in a rage," Wolfe said, oblivious to the emotions that roiled all around him. "A struggle ensued in the otherwise empty residence, and Alan Marx fell dead from an injury to his skull. Only young Mr. Hutchinson knows precisely what occurred and who initiated the fracas. I leave it to others to make that determination."

The room had become an emotional shambles. Various Hutchinsons embraced one another, and several were in tears. Kathleen hugged Cordelia, and Tom wrapped his arms around his mother, who sobbed into his chest.

All the bluster had gone out of Parkhurst, who sat slumped in his chair, staring at the floor. Marlene Peters had apparently become a pariah, as she was ignored.

Purley Stebbins led Doug out of the room while Cramer paused at the big desk, looking down at Wolfe. "We still have things to discuss," he said. "But they can wait—at least until tomorrow." As he walked out, I followed him down the hall in my sometime role as butler. I held the front door open for him, but got neither a look nor any thanks—not that I expected either.

When I got back to the office, Parkhurst Hutchinson sat in the red leather chair recently occupied by Cordelia and leaned forward, speaking in a low voice. "I can pay you the balance right now if you like," he said.

"That is not necessary. Mr. Goodwin will send you a bill."

"Mr. Wolfe, you warned me when I hired you that you might find things that were distasteful, unpleasant, and embarrassing to me and my family. I remember your precise wording. You were certainly correct about that."

"It gives me no satisfaction to be proven right," Wolfe said.

"I have been too hard on Doug these last few years," Hutchinson said, still keeping his voice low. "I blame myself for all that has happened, and I will spend whatever it takes to get the finest legal minds in this city to defend my son."

"Your son must shoulder some of the blame himself," Wolfe observed. "He is an intelligent adult and is possessed, as we all are, of free will."

Those words offered no solace to Parkhurst Hutchinson, who turned toward his wife. She was standing, surrounded by her three daughters and her eldest son, who together formed a protective cocoon around her. They made an opening in that cocoon for their father, who joined them in encircling and consoling a grieving woman.

I looked around for Marlene Peters, but she must have slipped out when I was eavesdropping on the conversation between Wolfe and Parkhurst Hutchinson. She was now probably walking along Thirty-Fifth Street, alone with her thoughts of what might have been.

CHAPTER 27

The next morning, true to form, Inspector Cramer arrived at the brownstone shortly after eleven. After getting the okay from Wolfe, I let him in. My smile was met with a grim nod as he walked by me toward the office. After settling into the red chair and pulling out an unlit cigar, the inspector looked at Wolfe and shook his head. "I don't know whether to thank you or tell you to go to hell," he said.

"Indeed a quandary," Wolfe replied. "I'm afraid I am not in a position to counsel you. Would you like something to drink? Coffee, perhaps? Beer?"

Cramer waved the offer away with his stogie. "The Hutchinson kid—hell, he's hardly a kid, is he?—spilled his guts at the station this morning without much prompting. His father got him a lawyer—a damned good one, too, one of the best in town—but young Hutchinson wouldn't listen to the mouthpiece's advice. He babbled like a magpie, and some of what he said might even be true."

"I am surprised," Wolfe said. "He seemed so truculent here that I supposed he would stubbornly deny everything."

"No, he caved in, totally. I think he saw how devastated his young sister was last night when she learned of his betrayal of her, and he had no fight left in him, none at all."

"Did he tell you how he and Alan Marx met?"

"Yes, he did. Say, that beer of yours looks good. If it's not too much of an imposition, I wouldn't mind some after all."

Wolfe pushed the buzzer on the underside of his desk, using the long-short-long signal that indicated to Fritz that a guest wanted a beer.

"Anyway," Cramer continued, "Hutchinson said he met Marx about a year ago at an art gallery party someplace down in the Village."

"I had suspected as much. This was hardly surprising, given that Marx was a collector and young Hutchinson is an artist, albeit one said to possess mediocre abilities."

"Yeah, well, I wouldn't know about that. Anyway, they got to talking, and Hutchinson confided that he had been in financial trouble ever since his former college classmate's import-export scheme had gone bust and his father had cut him off from any further family money. That first conversation led to others, with Marx learning more each time about the Hutchinson clan, particularly Cordelia and all her money." The inspector paused to drink from the beer Fritz had brought in and placed it on the small table next to him.

"Eventually, the two of them, with Marx being the mastermind, hit on the blackmail scheme, but they needed an accomplice. Enter Marlene Peters. She and Doug had been carrying on quietly for some time after their supposed breakup, with her pushing him to make more money so they could get married.

"Well, it seems that you know a lot of this already," Cramer continued, "but Marlene persuaded her friend Cordelia to go to

Italy, saying she would also be there. In fact, Marlene made sure to get there first, hooking up with Carlo Veronese and bringing him into the scheme. She had met this Veronese on a previous trip to Florence. By the way, that was one sweet stunt of yours, having Veronese step into the room at the key moment. That unnerved the hell out of everybody." Wolfe dipped his chin in acknowledgment.

"According to young Hutchinson during his babbling, Marlene got Veronese to agree to romance Cordelia and get pictures of them embracing in that park to make her fiancé back home jealous and get him to propose."

"Even though he—Lance Mercer by name—had already proposed to her," I put in.

"Yeah, I can't decide which of them was slimier—young Hutchinson or Marlene," Cramer said. "Veronese was slimy, too, of course, but at least he could fall back on the excuse, lame as it is, that he was doing this as a way to bring two young people together."

"So, how did Alan Marx get young Hutchinson to buy into the plan to kill me?" I asked.

"Oh yeah, here is what—by the way, how are you?" the inspector asked, turning to me with a look of genuine concern, probably the first one he had ever thrown my way.

"Healing nicely," I said. "Thanks for asking."

"Good. Here is what Douglas Hutchinson told us this morning. He swore, for what it's worth, that he had no idea murder was in the plans for the Central Park money drop. He claims he asked Marx what was in all this for him, and Marx told him he didn't like Nero Wolfe—although he didn't specify a reason—and was going to play a trick on him by making his assistant, Goodwin, be a party to the blackmailing."

"And what if we hadn't gone along with all of this?" I asked.

"I posed that question to young Hutchinson, and he told us he hadn't thought about it," Cramer said.

"Rubbish," Wolfe growled.

"I agree," Cramer said. "An awful lot of what this guy has been feeding us may well be rubbish. Including what happened later at Marx's co-op. He says he was still stunned by what he saw in the park from his vantage just west of the drop-off point for the money. First McManus shoots Goodwin and then Marx plugs McManus in the back. And to top it off, the money gets spirited away—by Durkin, you said."

"Yes, Fred brought the money here—all of it," Wolfe replied.

"The two men screamed at each other briefly in the park," Cramer continued, "but then they knew they had to get the hell out of there before squad cars came, which they did, going their separate ways.

"Doug Hutchinson said he brooded all night and into the next day, and then the next night, he went to Alan Marx's place and the two got into a shouting match all over again. Hutchinson says Marx swung the fireplace poker at him and they struggled over it, and somehow, Marx got hit hard, very hard, and fell on the floor, and Hutchinson panicked, running out and leaving by a back entrance and into a passageway behind the building."

"An implausible scenario," Wolfe remarked.

"Isn't it?" Cramer said. "Unfortunately, there were no witnesses, so there is only Hutchinson's version, which doesn't make him look very good. If I were his lawyer, I'd go for a manslaughter plea."

"Assuming he pays any attention to his lawyer," I said.

"That's his problem," Cramer said with a snort, before taking another sip of beer and licking his lips. "You tipped off your pal at the *Gazette*," he said to me.

I nodded. "Old friends, old loyalties."

"Cohen and I talked this morning. I assume there will be an item in the afternoon edition," he said. "It probably won't have Hutchinson's name in it, though. At least I didn't give it to him."

"Neither did I, Inspector. I just suggested he call you, and said that there was a development in the Marx murder. And I told him Mr. Wolfe wanted his name left out of it."

"Very noble of you both, I am sure," Cramer said, turning back to Wolfe. "I assume it was your sawbones down the block—what's-his-name—Vollmer, who patched Goodwin up."

"Mr. Goodwin was tended to by a doctor in New Jersey," Wolfe said with a straight face.

"Which, of course, is outside of my jurisdiction," Cramer remarked. "I get it. Well, if that's your story, who am I to contradict you? You've done what you damn well please all the way through this whole messy business anyway. What's one more nose-thumbing at the law?"

"You have your murderers, sir," Wolfe said.

"One of whom is dead. Well, I had better go out and grab a copy of the *Gazette* to see how badly Cohen butchered my quotes," the inspector said, rising slowly. "Thanks for the beer."

"There is a man who bears the burdens of the world on his shoulders," I said, returning to the office after having seen Cramer out.

"Or so he would have one believe," Wolfe said. "Mr. Cramer is used to complaining when he is here, but this time he does not have a great deal to be unhappy about."

"I suppose not. And the *Gazette* piece will likely make him look good. Lon has a lot of respect, albeit grudging, for the inspector. Say, I would like to know more about Saul's trip to Italy, unless that's privileged information."

Wolfe's cheeks creased again. At this rate, he would get a

record for smiles on a single case. "I gave him a simple assignment: Fly to Italy, find Carlo Veronese, persuade him to come to New York, and return here with him by the fastest means possible."

"Nothing to it. Cramer is right that Carlo's appearance here was a dandy stunt that knocked everyone for a loop. Those two left here last night before I had a chance to talk to them. Got an idea where Veronese is now?"

"Saul was to check him into a hotel, the Churchill, I believe, for two nights. Mr. Veronese had wanted a chance to see something of New York, as he had never been here before. I approved the expense, which, along with their airfares, will be added to Parkhurst Hutchinson's bill."

"As well it should," I said. "He can pay us out of his petty cash account. I doubt if he is happy with the outcome, though."

"Surely not. 'Uneasy lies the head that wears a crown.'"

"Sounds like it could be Shakespeare."

"*Henry IV, Part II*," Wolfe said.

"Well, maybe that also applies to Parkhurst the First."

"Money has purchased many things for the kingly Mr. Hutchinson, but happiness does not appear to be one of them."

In case you are wondering, that very night I did tell Wolfe about Annie Hutchinson's idea that he be the advertising face of Remmers Beer. "Unthinkable!" he exploded. When I handed him a sheet on which the amount he would have been paid was written, Wolfe was speechless.

When he finally found his voice, he turned to me and said, "Archie, please call Annie Hutchinson and tell her she has lost control of her senses."

Needless to say, I never made that call.

CHAPTER 28

For the record, the *Gazette* and our friend Lon Cohen gave all the credit in the solving of the murders of McManus and Marx to Inspector Lionel T. Cramer of the New York Police Department's Homicide Squad. Nero Wolfe's name did not appear in the story, as we had requested. And if you are wondering, Parkhurst Hutchinson paid Wolfe's bill without a peep, despite the considerable expense involved in bringing Carlo Veronese to New York.

As of this writing, the case of the State of New York v. Douglas Hutchinson has yet to be resolved. The Hutchinson lawyers pressed for a manslaughter charge in the death of Alan Marx, but the New York County District Attorney is going for a first-degree murder charge, and there have been numerous continuances.

The other day I had lunch with Tom Hutchinson, who insisted on reciprocating for my treating him at La Belle Touraine by buying me lunch there. "Archie, I just got a good promotion at work, and I'm seeing a really nice woman now," he said with a smile over cocktails. "I want you to know that I really appreciate the way you and your boss handled things for our family during a rough period."

He went on to tell me that Cordelia and Lance Mercer had called off their engagement, although he was unsure as to whose idea it was. He said Cordelia had decided to go back to Europe to study Renaissance art at a school in some Italian town, the name of which I forget—it was not Florence. She planned to stay for at least two years, he said.

He told me his sister Annie had found herself a new friend, an art director at a competing advertising agency, and he felt she was now happier than she had been in years.

"I'm not sure what will come of it over time," he said, "but I've met the guy, and he seems to be solid, which is more than I can say for some of the men she's been with in the past."

I asked about Kathleen, whom I had driven up to Connecticut to see. "She's about the same, Archie. If I were a violent man, I would have killed that bum she was married to, but"—he shrugged—"he's really not worth the effort. She has been a wonderful mother to those little girls, but she has pretty much sacrificed any private life she has for them.

"As far as my folks," he went on, "they have not been the same since what has happened with Doug, and I doubt if they ever will be. My mother has turned in on herself, never goes out anymore, and does not want to see anyone—not that she ever was that social a person. And my father has pretty much lost interest in the railroad that he helped make into a national powerhouse. He just doesn't seem to care anymore, and he says that he's going to resign the chairmanship and leave the board at the end of the year."

When I queried him about Marlene Peters, Tom shook his head. "I don't know what has become of her, and I don't care. But I can tell you this: When the police were talking about charging

Marlene as an accessory in the blackmailing, Cordelia stepped in, claiming they were good friends and she—Cordelia—said it was all just a big misunderstanding. I was very proud of her, but I had to wonder how things would have turned out had their roles been reversed. Some friend to my sister Miss Marlene Peters turned out to be!"

I told Tom I was sorry about the family's misfortunes but happy for him and his sister Annie. After lunch, we shook hands out on the sun-drenched sidewalk in front of the restaurant and went our separate ways. I turned to look at his back as he headed in the other direction, noting a bounce in his step I had not seen before.

As for myself, I got the last of my bandages off this week. Doc Vollmer's comely nurse, Carol Francis, came over to the brownstone, unwrapped me yet again, studied my healed wound, and pronounced me fit.

"Try to behave yourself from now on," she cautioned. I promised I would and we embraced—like brother and sister.

Last night, Lily Rowan and I went dancing at the Flamingo Club, but hardly like brother and sister. "You seem to be much more relaxed tonight, Escamillo," she said as she pressed her cheek against mine.

"Really? I thought I was always relaxed."

"Not the last time we went dancing, a couple of weeks ago," she told me. "You seemed all tensed up, like your shoulder was bothering you, although I didn't say anything about it and you didn't mention it."

"Oh, yeah, I do remember. That was because I had pulled a muscle doing my morning exercises a while back."

"Well, please try to be more careful in the future, will you? I have always said that exercising can be dangerous to one's health."

AUTHOR NOTES

This story is set in the middle of the twentieth century, during the Truman Administration and the Korean War.

Some comments about persons and places referred to in the narrative:

Stan Musial of the St. Louis Cardinals, whom Archie watches in awe when he attends a game between the Cardinals and the New York Giants at the Polo Grounds in Manhattan, has been a member of the Baseball Hall of Fame since 1969, and was arguably baseball's premier player in the Mid-Century era, having played in twenty-four All-Star games and four World Series, and having won seven National League batting championships. His lifetime batting average of .331 places him in the top thirty all-time players.

The Merritt Parkway, which Archie uses on his drive to Connecticut to visit Kathleen Willis, is an historic, limited-access road built between 1934 and 1940, and in part because of its tree-lined and billboard-free setting, it is listed on the National Register of Historic Places. It runs from the New York–Connecticut border thirty-seven miles east, spanning the width of Fairfield County.

AUTHOR NOTES

Westport, Connecticut, where Kathleen Willis lives, is a coastal town forty-seven miles northeast of New York City, and has long been one of the wealthiest communities in the United States.

Work on the **United Nations Building**, which Archie passes on a walk around Manhattan, began in 1948 and was still under construction at the time of this story. The core complex was completed in 1952.

The fictional **Mason's Book Nook**, where Archie meets Marlene Peters, is located in what is now known as Manhattan's **East Village**, as is Miss Peters' apartment, but because that term for the neighborhood did not exist in the 1950s, I refer to the area simply as the **Lower East Side**.

La Belle Touraine restaurant in Manhattan, where Archie has lunch with Tom Hutchinson, is fictional also, although its interior layout is loosely based on the designs of several Midtown restaurants where I have eaten over the years.

Gerald's Public House in Midtown Manhattan, where Archie has drinks and dinner with Annie Hutchinson, is fictional as well, but is loosely based on a couple of New York pubs I have visited.

As with my previous Wolfe novels, my heartfelt thanks go to Barbara Stout and Rebecca Stout Bradbury for their continued support and encouragement.

My warm thanks and appreciation also go to my agent, Martha Kaplan; to Otto Penzler and Rob Hart of Mysterious Press; and to Nina Lassam and Hannah Dudley, along with others on the team at Open Road Integrated Media. You have all given wise counsel that has helped to smooth our rough spots at various points along the way.

And most of all, my thanks and love to my wife, Janet, to whom this book is dedicated and who has always been a steadying influence on both my work and my life.

ABOUT THE AUTHOR

Robert Goldsborough is an American author best known for continuing Rex Stout's famous Nero Wolfe series. Born in Chicago, he attended Northwestern University and upon graduation went to work for the *Associated Press*, beginning a lifelong career in journalism that would include long periods at the *Chicago Tribune* and *Advertising Age*. While at the *Tribune*, Goldsborough began writing mysteries in the voice of Rex Stout, the creator of iconic sleuths Nero Wolfe and Archie Goodwin. Goldsborough's first novel starring Wolfe, *Murder in E Minor* (1986), was met with acclaim from both critics and devoted fans, winning a Nero Award from the Wolfe Pack.

MYSTERIOUSPRESS.COM

Otto Penzler, owner of the Mysterious Bookshop in Manhattan, founded the Mysterious Press in 1975. Penzler quickly became known for his outstanding selection of mystery, crime, and suspense books, both from his imprint and in his store. The imprint was devoted to printing the best books in these genres, using fine paper and top dust-jacket artists, as well as offering many limited, signed editions.

Now the Mysterious Press has gone digital, publishing ebooks through **MysteriousPress.com**.

MysteriousPress.com offers readers essential noir and suspense fiction, hard-boiled crime novels, and the latest thrillers from both debut authors and mystery masters. Discover classics and new voices, all from one legendary source.